To Bet

The Adventures Of a Jackabee

From Malcolm.

Hope you enjoy

Published by
Impression Publishing
www.impressionpublishing.net

First Edition published 2012

Printed and bound in Great Britain by
printmyownbook.com

A catalogue record for this book
is available from The British Library
ISBN 978-1-908374-67-7

Mr Hoggs came in late as usual for his meal. He had been working on a big job in the factory. His wife Mary was a loving person, very gentle and concerned about her husband. She quickly heated his dinner, which she had prepared over an hour ago, and set it down at the table where he sat. Mary took a little for herself, and asked how things had gone at work that day. She knew the answer before she asked the question.

"Oh just the same old stuff," came the reply.

Mary was concerned about her husband, because she knew he was very worried about their lack of money, and he was not keeping very well either. But he did try his best to keep all the family fed and in warm clothes.

She knew he worked far too hard for a man sixty years old. When he was tired he had a very bad temper. Mr Hoggs did not mean to shout at his wife or children. He was really a very good man, and if he did shout, he was very sorry afterwards.

At number 19 Roundtree Road also lived their three children. Maryann who was seven and a half. Maryann was very proud of that half, and would tell everybody in a cheeky little voice,

"I am seven and a big half."

Then came Rose, who had just turned four, and little Johnny who was almost three. Last, but by no means least, was Bea, a scruffy two year old Beagle. Bea was the family pet. They all loved her. But Mr Hoggs was always complaining about buying food for her.

"Dog meat is expensive now days. We would have more food for ourselves, if it wasn't for that dog. How did it get in here anyway?" he would say.

Knowing full well that Maryann had been feeding the dog at the back door because it had no home. Then when winter came Mr Hoggs allowed it to come inside.

"Just for a little while," he would say.

But little by little it edged its way in until it got as close to the fire as the rest of the family, and there it stayed.

Just before Christmas that year Mr Hoggs got some bad news from his employer.

"We're going to have to ask you to leave Tom.

There is not enough work for us now. We know

you're a good worker Tom, but times are hard," said John the boss.

"I am very, very sorry. Here are a few weeks' wages. Maybe that will help you over Christmas," he continued.

"OK, OK. I get it," said Tom.

"As if I didn't have enough trouble. Three kids to feed and that useless dog. It has a better life than I do." Tom left and went for a long walk to think things through.

He arrived home at one am, in a very bad mood. Everyone else had gone to bed, except Bea who was eating from her bowl in the kitchen.

Tom started to shout at Bea, "It's all right for you. You just eat and sleep all day. I have to go to work to feed you."

He really lost his temper, opened the back door, grabbed Bea by the collar, and threw her outside, shouting, "Go and look after yourself. Get a job, you scruffy lazy dog."

Later that night Mr Hoggs felt very sorry he had thrown Bea out. He looked for her outside, but she had gone.

It was a cold night. Bea had been a stray dog before. She knew what it was like to be unwanted and unloved. However, she took comfort in knowing that all the other members of the family did love her. She knew that Mr Hoggs was fond of her too, in his own way, but he was very worried about lots of things which were going wrong. She did not totally understand what was happening, but she could hear lots of shouting and arguing in the home. She knew something was not right.

"I will stay away for a few days," she thought.

"Then I'll go back when things have calmed down a bit." Bea spent the first night in an old upturned bin, which had blown over in the wind the night before.

"I am lucky he did not throw me out last night. At least, though it is cold, the wind has died down to a gentle breeze." But Bea thought it must be coming from Iceland as it was so cold! Bea then thought about Iceland.

"That's where Father Christmas lives." She thought about Christmas. The smell of turkey, stuffing, pork sausages and maybe some chicken cooking. A tear came to her eye.

"If I can't get home again, and can find no one to take me in, there will be no Christmas for me this year. I will be searching the bins again for bits of scraps. There will be no Christmas presents from Santa."

That was an even worse thought. Bea was cold. She found an old coat which somebody had thrown into the entry. She dragged the coat into her bin and closed her eyes. Tired and exhausted from her ordeal, she soon fell asleep.

BEA GETS HUNGRY

About two streets away from where Bea was there was a grand park, with tall trees and bushy bushes. Some were still green even though it was six weeks to Christmas. Some were a little white from the frost, but that did not matter to Jack. He was running really fast, rolling in the little snow that had fallen, and chasing the leaves that danced in the wind. Jack was a tough little character. Jack was a Pedigree Jack Russell. He had won many shows for his appearance and intelligence. Although small, Jack was fearless.

Other dogs knew Jack, and behaved with respect towards him - even the big ones! Jack's owner was called Richard; a tall man, strong and also fearless. He and Jack walked everywhere together. They really loved each other. Richard would care for Jack, and Jack would walk proudly along side him, thinking, "This is my master and friend. Dare anybody come too close and they will be in big trouble." But there were times when Jack would have liked to have a little female dog to love too. So he would slip out some nights, when Richard fell asleep in front of the fire. Jack would never go too far, because he would worry that he may not hear his master calling him if he woke up and needed Jack. That was why he always stayed in his own garden. And because of that he never met any nice female dogs to fall in love with.

Meanwhile, Bea had wakened in her upturned bin and looked outside. The old coat had kept her warm through the night. She smelt the air. Somebody was cooking sausages and bacon for breakfast.

"Oh, she thought, it would be so nice to have some of that." She followed the smell carefully until it brought her to a brightly coloured back door. The smell was really intense now, and Bea's mouth began to water. She could almost taste the sausage and bacon.

Bea thought, "How can I let the person know that I feel so hungry? I know, I will scrape on the door like I used to do back home." Bea stood up on her back legs, and with her front paws scraped at the door. She tried once, and then stopped, but no one opened the door.

"I will try again," she said to herself. Again and

again Bea tried. She scraped harder, until some of the brightly coloured paint came off the door unto her paws. Suddenly the door opened, and there stood an old woman in a black coat. Her hair was gray and black.

"She looks scary," thought Bea, who then took a step back.

"What do you think you are doing to my lovely door?" bellowed the old woman.

"Go away you dirty, scruffy, mongrel dog. You are smelly, and your coat is all matted."

At this, she grabbed a yard brush and tried to hit Bea with it. Bea was getting really angry, not so much because the old witch had called Bea dirty and smelly, but because she had called her a mongrel dog.

"I am NOT a Mongrel Dog!" she told the witch. In dog language that sounded something like BARK, BBBBARK, BARK, GROWL, BARK.

Of course the old woman was not a witch but just looked like one to Bea.

Bea thought to herself, "You would be smelly and dirty too if you had to sleep in a bin at night. All I wanted was a little food." Bea ran away disgusted with the old woman.

Some hours later she found a scrap of meat on the footpath, she ate it so quickly it gave her pains in her stomach. She remembered, when she was a pup, her mother always told her not to gulp her food, because it was bad for her to do that. Also, never ever bark when eating. That was very rude. Bea had been well brought up in a very posh part of town. She could bark very politely when she wanted to. But when she was very young, her mummy died, and the people who owned the fancy house moved away to an apartment. Bea was left to fend for herself. Bea always took care of her coat and groomed every morning and night, but because of what had happened to her she really looked terrible! Just like a scruffy old mongrel. Just like the horrible old woman had said. Night was beginning to fall.

Bea thought to herself, "I must find shelter soon. It's going to be very cold tonight again. There may even be some more snow, I heard some humans say to each other." She crawled through a hedge. By this time she was completely lost. She saw a shed where someone had left the door open a little.

"Maybe I could spend the night in there." Bea was starving, but happy to find that the shed was warm and dry. There were some old clothes lying on the floor, and a well chewed dog bone. Bea thought, "I must not steal some other dog's bone. That would not be right." But when she looked more closely, there was no meat left on it anyway. Bea took the bone between her teeth. She pretended it had lots of succulent juicy meat still on it. She fell asleep with the bone still in her mouth.

BEA MEETS JACK

Bea woke with a start, to the sound of barking. It was Jack standing over her, and he was not very pleased. "What are you doing in here? Why are you eating my bone? Who said you could come into my shed? How long have you been here? How dare you!" Bea stopped him before he could say any more. (All of this was dog language of course Bark - BbbbbBBBark -growl - Bark - bark etc.) "I am so sorry," she said.

"Huh," said Jack. "Sorry nothing." Pack your bags and get out before I throw you out."

Bea cried a little. "I am so hungry, I have been put out of my home, and nobody will give me any food. I only wanted to keep warm for the night. Besides, there was no meat left on the bone anyway."

Bea got up to her feet. She was so weak that she fell back down again. Jack looked at her and started to feel a little bit sorry. Jack was well looked after. He had lots of food whenever he wanted it.

"Stay there a while. I will bring you some food and

then you will have to go," said Jack.

Jack went into the house. Richard was still asleep because it was only two o'clock in the morning. Jack had been out in the garden, hoping to find a nice lady dog for himself. However he definitely did NOT fancy Bea. She was scruffy and smelly, and had no decent upbringing.

"Not good enough for a Pedigree Jack Russell like me," Jack thought.

Jack found some tasty dog biscuits Richard had left on a low shelf in the kitchen. He put four into his mouth. Being very careful not to chew them, he brought them to the shed where Bea was waiting. Bea almost dived on him to get at the food. She gulped them down, saying at the same time,

"Thank you so much." After she had finished the biscuits, Bea remembered what her mother had told her. "Never speak with your mouth full, it is very rude."

"Oh, I am so sorry for being rude, by speaking to you while I was eating. Please forgive me. I was just so hungry."

Jack looked at her in amazement and said to her

"What would you know about being rude? You are just a smelly old mongrel, not a proper pedigree like I am."

Bea was furious! "I am not a smelly old mongrel. I am a well bred pedigree Beagle. I know my manners. I lived in the most posh part of town until my mother died, when I was young. I am smelly because I have had to sleep in a bin all last night. Not like you. You are a pompous, ill-mannered dog, who has everything. I really do not like you!" she shouted at Jack. "I am going now and I won't be back. GOODBYE"! Bea said in the loudest bark she ever heard. It was so loud that she even frightened herself.

Jack stood looking at her. He was amazed that she had stood up to him. Most other dogs would have run away, if they thought Jack was angry.

"Wait a minute", Jack said, "Maybe I was a bit hasty. Look, I will show you where the bath is, and you can have a good wash, and comb that fur before my master gets up".

Bea settled down. The thought of a nice bath, and to be able to comb her fur was so good, she just could not resist it.

She said "OK, but then I will be on my way."

BEA GETS A BATH

Jack showed her into another shed, nearer the house. "There," he said, and pointed to an old tin bath in the corner, "I will run the hose and make it nice and hot for you. Over there is a brush and a comb and some of that bath shampoo. I hate it myself, but I suppose you being a girl will love it!"

"Yuck," Jack murmured under his breath. Jack filled the bath and turned off the water. "Right", he said, "Get in now."

Bea looked at him. "Not with you standing there," she said. "You be a gentleman dog, and go outside. Don't look until I am finished, then I will call you in."

It felt like hours. Jack thought, "Why can't they just have a quick shower like any dog would? Huh, lady dogs. Hours in the bath."

He was about to peep in and see if Bea was ready, but remembering his manners just in time, he did not.

Then he heard Bea call, "OK, you can come in

now."

Jack opened the door. He stood there with his eyes wide open. He wiped his eyes with his paws, because he thought he was seeing things. There, in front of him, was the most attractive female dog he had ever seen! Jack fell in love with Bea at that moment and Bea knew it.

"You really are a pedigree," said Jack. Bea had combed her fur well and fixed her hair really nicely. She also had on lots of that shampoo stuff, as Jack calls it. "You look beautiful, and you smell lovely too for a girl dog. That stuff is OK on you girls, but not on us men dogs. We are too tough to go around smelling like that." "You know" said Jack "I think the best Shampoo is a good roll in some horse poo in the fields."

"Don't be crude," said Bea". "Remember you are a pedigree".
"O yes I know," said Jack. "But sometimes I just want to be like other dogs and have a bit of fun."

"Well," said Bea "I better be on my way now. I did say after my bath I would go away and not come back." "Aaa! Just don't be too hasty Bea," said Jack trying not to let her know he had gone soft on

her. "I could talk to Richard and maybe he might let you stay a while, just a little while until you get somewhere of your own you understand." Jack had no intentions of letting her go away. A pretty girl dog of his own and a pedigree as well, is what he always wanted. Jack was well pleased.

BEA MEETS RICHARD.

"Now, let's see," thought Jack. What would be the best time to tell my master about Bea?" Jack knew that Richard was always in a good mood after dinner. "Dinner," Jack said aloud.

"Do you want some dinner Bea? I am so sorry, I forgot to ask you if you were hungry."

"Yes," said Bea, I am rather peckish." pretending to be polite. She was starving again.

Remember all she had eaten were four dog biscuits. Jack crossed the garden to the old vegetable patch. It was covered in a light skiff of snow. Jack was cold, but would not let Bea see him shivering. Jack always wanted to be rough and look tough. He started to dig. After a few minutes he was down as far as his legs would go. He pulled up a bone; a really good bone that he had hidden a week or two ago.

"Better to bury your bone for a week or so," he told Bea, as he gave it to her to eat. "Gives it a bit more flavour!" he said, with great authority on all bones and the like. There was lots of meat, fat, and

grizzle on this bone. Bea looked at Jack saying,

"I can't take this - it is far too good for you to give away."

"Don't worry," Jack said, "I have lots like that hidden around the garden." Jack didn't really have another bone like that one. It was his prize one that he was keeping for a special dinner for himself. But he was happy to let Bea have it, to show her how much he really cared for her.

Bea chewed and gnawed at that bone for almost two hours. She was so happy it pleased Jack to see the smile on her face. Jack really loved Bea now, and wanted to do lots of good things for her. He wanted to please her, and look after her forever. They played in the snow around the garden until it was getting dark.

Neither of them had noticed the time passing. They heard a loud voice coming from the house. "Jack! Jack! Come here. It is time for your walk in the park "Oh dear!" Jack said, "I will have to go. Run into the shed and wait for me I will be back soon." Bea did as she was told. "I will be a good dog and keep my master in a good mood for tonight, when I tell him about you."

"Bye, bye," said Bea. Hurry back soon, I am missing you already." Jack beamed, and held his head high and his chest out.

"I have my own lady dog now." he thought.

When they returned Jack went to collect Bea from the shed.

"OK," he said. "It's now or never. Come with me." Jack opened the dog flap on the back door. Like a gentleman dog he held it open for Bea. "Now Bea please be quiet. I will see if he is awake." Richard had just settled down in his favorite armchair, and looked very comfortable and content sitting with his cup of cocoa.

Jack wondered should he jump on to his knee and tell him. "Maybe not, that might scare him, and he might get cross. Shall I sneak up and lick his hand? Oh, I don't know - that might make him jump." Jack was wandering around the room wondering what to do, when Richard said,

"Come here Jack. What's the matter boy, you look as if you want to tell me something." Jack stopped immediately. He looked up at his master and wagged his tail.

He then ran into the kitchen and told Bea to follow him. Bea did as she was told. Richard looked down at Bea. He was very tall and Bea could hardly see his face.

"What's this?" he asked Jack. A lady friend you have brought to meet me?" (Jack could understand every word - as most dogs do, without their masters knowing.) Jack wagged his tail, and went over to Bea and licked her nose. "I see," said Richard, "You have fallen in love with this lovely little Beagle dog. She can stay with us as long as she wants."

The two dogs jumped on to Richard's knee as soon as he sat down again, trying to lick his face and his hands, until Richard said, "Enough, enough Jack. Take Bea and show her around the house, like a good gentleman dog would do with such a nice lady dog." Jack and Bea were very happy.

JACK ASKS BEA TO MARRY HIM

Jack and Bea had been together now for almost six months and Jack thought it was time to ask Bea to marry him. Jack wondered what the best way of doing this was, because he wanted to make a really good impression on her, in case she might say no. Jack looked around for the biggest juiciest bone he could find to give to her.

This was the dogs' way of proposing. Instead of giving a diamond ring, a dog always gives it's best bone. That shows her how much he loves her. He then took a bath. Jack hated baths. He would roll in all sorts of strange things during the day which he thought made him really manly - a real tough dog smell. But a bath!! "Oh well, I suppose to please Bea I will do it. But just this once!" he thought.

Jack pulled a bunch of beautiful daises and dandelions and set them beside the bone in the garden. He then ran to find Bea. She was busy in the dog shed tiding up last night's mess that they had both made when eating their dinner.

"Bea," shouted Jack. "Come here. I have something to show you."

"OK," said Bea. "I will be with you in a minute." Jack ran back up the garden to where he had the bone and flowers laid out on the grass. He could not wait. He shouted again,

"Come on Bea!"

"Alright! Alright I am coming." Bea barked back. Bea did not like to be rushed, but she could sense the urgency in Jack's voice, so she ran up to where he was standing.

"What's all the fuss about Jack?" asked Bea. Then she saw the bone and the way that he had arranged the flowers. She knew what Jack was going to say.

"Bea," said Jack as he knelt down on his two front paws. "Bea," he said again. This time there was a little quiver in his bark. Jack had never felt so nervous. He had fought with big dogs, he had chased off a fox once, but never had he felt like this! "BEA," he almost shouted, "Will you marry me?" Bea did not even have to think about the answer.

"YES! YES! YES!" She shouted back, "I will. I love you so much, and we will have lots of puppies just like you Jack." Jack was very happy. He said, "We will tell all the dogs in the neighbourhood to come to the wedding. We are going to have the biggest dog wedding ever. With lots and lots of meat and juicy bones for everyone.

THE TWO MEET BOXER

Later that evening Bea looked over at Jack as they lay in the dog house. "Jack, it is great to be having a big wedding and all the trimmings, but who is going to marry us?"

Jack looked over at her, "Why Bea, I never thought of that. Tomorrow we will ask Boxer," Jack said.

Boxer was an old dog. He was about 10 years old. Now 10 years old in dog years is 70 years old in human years. Boxer was very clever, he knew almost everything. All the dogs in the neighbourhood would go to him if they needed to know something.

Boxer would sit on his hind legs and look up at the sky as if he was waiting for an answer from heaven. He would then give himself a good scratch, look down at the ground, then at the dog that was asking the question, and usually gave a very good answer.

The next morning right after breakfast Jack and Bea set off to see Boxer. On the way they passed several dog friends who lived nearby.

"Hi Jack, Hi Bea," they would bark, "Where are you going, so early in the morning?"

"We are off to see Boxer," they barked back.

"We want to know who will marry us."

"Are you two getting married?" shouted Tiger.

Tiger was a tiny little mongrel, part Yorky and something else that nobody seemed to recognize. He had a few black stripes on his back, so his owners called him Tiger. Jack thought Pussy would have been a better name, because he was nothing like a Tiger. But Jack liked him anyway, and thought he would ask him to the wedding. "You can come to the wedding!" Jack barked to Tiger. "In fact all of you are invited. Bring all your friends as well. This is going to be the biggest wedding ever!"

Boxer was standing at the gate of his house, looking up and down the street, taking note of everything, because he always wanted to find out more and more. "Hello!" he said to Jack in a very deep bark.

"Hi Boxer," said Jack. "This is my friend Bea. We want to get married, but we don't know who will

marry us. Can you help Boxer?"

"You want to get married? Are you two not a bit young for marriage? You do know about puppies and all the responsibilities which they bring?"

"We love each other," said Bea. "And we can look after puppies. We really are old enough!" "Well," said Boxer, "Let me think."

Boxer looked up to the sky as usual and gave himself a big long scratch. Then he gave himself an extra scratch, not because the first scratch didn't help, but just because he enjoyed it so much. Boxer then, true to form, looked down to the ground, then back to Jack and Bea and said, "I think Great Dane is the only one who can marry you."

"Who is Great Dane?" they both asked together. Boxer started to look at the sky again. "Come on Boxer!" Just tell us who he is, and where he lives. Never mind all that looking at the sky stuff, we know you have the answer, and we haven't got time for all this."

"OK" said Boxer, a little put out at Jack's impatience, because Boxer liked to put on a little show before he gave an answer.

"Great Dane lives on the other side of town, where all the very posh people and their dogs live. I do not know which house or garden he lives in, but other dogs tell me it is so big you would think it was a park. There are high walls and gates. The house is so large it has 20 bedrooms. In there also live two Alsatians, who are very nasty and would bite any intruders. The owner of this property is a very wealthy man, who works in parliament, I believe. That's all I can tell you Jack. Good luck on your journey," said Boxer.

"And by the way I have a friend who might be able to help you. His name is Dal. Dal is a very beautiful and friendly Dalmatian. If you follow the river for about 10 miles, Dal lives in the red and blue house near the big oak tree. Tell him I sent you and he will help you find Great Dane. You will know Dal when you see him. He is tall and covered in black spots."

"Thank you so much," said Bea.

"Yea, thanks," said Jack. "We will be on our way now. Better get started as it seems we have a long journey ahead of us."

GREAT DANE

Jack and Bea set off along the river path, just as Boxer told them.

"We had better run," said Bea. "We have 10 miles to go to reach the red and blue house, to see Dal."

"Yes," said Jack, "We want to be back before dark or Richard will be worried about us and worse still we might miss our dinner!" Jack was always thinking of his stomach. They had travelled about five miles when the sky started to turn a bit dark.

"Oh dear," said Bea.

"It's going to rain, and I am getting tired and a bit hungry."

"Never mind," Jack said. "Let's stop a while over there. I can see an old shed where we can stay in out of the rain and rest a while. I will have a look around and see if I can find some food." Jack and Bea just got into the shed a minute befor [illegible] to rain and rain it did! It poured [illegible] thought he spotted a rabbit in the [illegible] made a run for it. The rabbit ran [illegible]

could, but Jack was a good hunter and soon caught up with his prey. One good bite on the back of the rabbit's neck did the trick. He trailed it back to share with Bea. They both enjoyed their feed, and about an hour later the rain was over.

"Let's go," said Bea. "I feel much better now."

They both set off again, running as fast as they could, jumping over felled trees and sliding in the mud and dirt left by the rain. Suddenly they saw in the distance a little old house with a red and blue fence.

"This must be where Dal lives," said Jack.

"Yes," said Bea. "Let's run to meet him."

"Careful," said Jack. "Let me go first, just in case there is any trouble." Jack wanted to protect Bea, and he liked to show her how brave he was. Jack walked slowly to the gate. He stopped and listened. There was no sound. He opened the gate and looked inside, but nobody was around.

"I had better call," he thought, "It is not right to go into another dog's property until you are invited. That's asking for trouble if you do that. Bark, Bark, Barkkkkk," Jack shouted, which meant

"Hello, anybody there?" There was no answer. Jack was not too sure what to do next. Should he go in and look around, or should he wait. "Better we wait," Bea said.

"Yes," agreed Jack. About half an hour passed before Jack saw this large white dog with lots of black spots coming up the lane beside the river. "Hello," he asked, "What can I do for you two? Sorry I was not in when you called. My master and I were doing a bit of fishing on the river." He spoke with a very posh accent.

"We have come to see if you can help us find Great Dane. Boxer sent us, he said you were his friend. We want to get married you see."

"I can tell you where to find Great Dane, but getting in to see him is another matter. Did Boxer tell you about the two Alsatians who guard the big house? They do not like any dog or anything to enter their garden. I could tell you lots of sad stories about some who tried. They got in OK, but were never seen again. I would not go anywhere near that place."

Great Dane is a good dog - very posh! But those other two - well they are trouble".

"Don't worry," said Jack, although he did feel a little frightened, but did not like to show it. "We will be OK. We want to get married, so we have to see Great Dane one way or the other."

"OK," said Dal. "Follow this road over that mountain until you see a sign at the cross roads pointing to a Castle. Follow that road. Great Dane lives in the Castle. But remember what I told you, many get in but nobody comes out!"

TO THE CASTLE

Jack and Bea thanked Dal for all his help. Dal asked them if they wanted to stay a while or share some food with him, but they said that they must get on before dark.

They ran on and Dal shouted after them, "It's another seven miles until you reach the sign post, and another three after that. Hope to see you both again on your way back, but I doubt it!!"

After running for about an hour they saw the sign post that pointed to the Castle, which they could see on the hill.

Jack said, "This is it Bea. Here we can get married."

"Oh! Jack, I am so frightened of these Alsatians."

"Don't be," said Jack. "I will take care of them and look after you."

Jack hadn't a clue how he was going to take care of two huge vicious Alsatians, but he was not frightened of them! Well, he pretended not to be anyway.

Jack stopped outside the fence of the Castle and listened. He could hear barking and growling from inside. He could hear two large dogs talking to each other. One was saying, "I wish someone would break in here tonight. I could do with some fresh meat."

"Yes," said the other one, "Me too." Jack did not tell Bea what he had heard because she was frightened enough already. Jack thought of a plan.

"They want meat, so then I will give them meat."

Jack told Bea of his plan to get inside.

"Oh dear Jack. What if it does not work?"

"Don't worry. It will. They are greedy dogs, just big and fat. They can't think like I can cause they are not as smart as I am."

Jack told Bea his plan and asked her to get ready to do what he needed. Jack then slipped through a small hole in the fence, before the Alsatians looked that way. He opened the gate with his teeth from the inside. The noise of the gate opening alerted the two dogs, who came bounding over to see what was happening. Jack ran as fast as he could though the open gate. The two dogs licked their lips and bounded after him through the gate, and into the forest nearby.

Bea carried out her part of the plan. She rushed into the Castle and closed the gate behind her. When Jack looked back he saw the gate was closed, but he also saw the two Alsatians almost on top of him, snapping, barking, and growling. In their rush to have more meat they had run straight out of the gate. Jack did a quick turn around. The big Alsatians couldn't turn as quickly as he could and that gave him a little advantage. His legs were sore because he had never run so fast in all his life, but this time his life depended on it. He could feel the hot breath of one of the Alsatians on his back.

"I must make it, I must," thought Jack. "Yes!!"

He could see the tiny hole in the fence that he was heading for. Snap, Snap, went the teeth of the Alsatians right behind Jack. Then, just as one of the dogs was about to bite Jack's back leg, he disappeared through the hole in the fence. The Alsatian was going so fast he could not stop, and almost knocked his own front teeth out when he hit the fence. The second dog ran into the first one and they both began to fight with each other about being so silly and falling into Jack's trap.

"Now," said Jack. "That's got rid of those two. Let's find Great Dane."

"Oh you are so brave!" said Bea.

JACK AND BEA MEET GREAT DANE

Jack and Bea walked up the long path towards the big house. When they got to the door Bea asked,

"What are we going to do Jack? The knocker is far too high for us to reach."

"Come with me round the back. There may be somebody about." Jack led the way slowly. He walked, looking around every corner with one eye before going any further. He was being very careful indeed. Suddenly, he heard someone shout, "Hello there. Who are you and what do you want?" Jack looked all around. He could not see anyone.

"Did you hear that Bea?"

"Yes I did," she said. "It sounded like a very deep voice." Again the voice said, "What do you want? It is dangerous around here."

"Where are you?" said Jack "I can't see you."

"Look up," the voice said. Jack and Bea looked up and there - almost standing beside them, was the biggest dog they had ever seen.

It was Great Dane. He was about ten times the size of Jack and Bea put together.

"Oh my," said Bea "You must be who we are looking for!"

"Yes I am," said the Great Dane. Jack was speechless.

"What do you want here?"

"We want to get married," said Jack eventually.

"We were told by Boxer that you were the only dog in this area who could marry us."

"Oh," said Great Dane. "Is that what you want? Then you must follow me into the yard to meet my master. By the way my name is Viking. What are your names?"

"I am Jack and this is Bea. We are two pedigrees you know. We have both been well brought up, and we know our manners."

"Glad to hear that," said Viking. "My master does not like unruly dogs."

"How did you get in here passed the guards?" "That was easy! Do you mean those silly pair, Bill and Ben the Alsatians?" asked Jack.

"Yes," said Viking.

"Well I think they are still outside, trying to get back in." Viking laughed "Yes," he said. "Not too many brains in those two. The master will not be too pleased with them."

Every now and again Viking had to stop and wait for Jack and Bea. Although he was just walking normally they were having to run. They just could not keep up with him.

Finally they all reached the big house. Viking pushed the bell with his paw; he could reach it easily. The door opened, and the butler said,

"Come in Viking, and please bring your two friends with you, I will tell the master you are here." The master entered the room. Viking sat down, and told the others to do the same.

"Well Viking, I see you have some friends with you. Where are the guards? How did they get in here?"

Viking looked towards the gate, the two silly Alsatians were jumping up and down outside.

"A lot of use they are!" said the Master. "I will be going on business tomorrow," he told Viking.

"Why don't you ask your friends to stay a day or two? Show them round a bit." Viking thought that this was a great opportunity to have a grand wedding in the big hall, while the master was away.

THE BIG WEDDING

When the Master left the room, Viking said to Jack and Bea, "How would you two like to get married here in the great hall? You could bring all your friends, and I will talk to the head chef about some dinner for you all."

"That would be wonderful!" they both barked at the same time. "You are so good to us," said Bea.

"Well," said Viking, "It's a long time since we had a good party here, and I will be happy to marry you both as soon as we can arrange it. We only have a few days until the Master comes back from London, so let's get started. You two run off now and tell all your friends to come here tomorrow at noon, and we will have everything ready."

"Great," said Bea, "But what about the two Alsatians? Won't they be cross when they see all the dogs coming to the Castle?"

"Never you mind about them," said Viking. "They do as I say! I will be keeping them busy, serving the food, and then they can do all the washing up."

Jack and Bea laughed.

"Serves them right," said Bea, "for being so stupid."

Jack and Bea thanked Viking again and again. "Run on now you two, and tell all your friends on the way home."

Off they went in a real flurry of excitement. When they came to the gate the two Alsatians were waiting outside. "Let us in," one of them barked angrily.

"Not until you say please, and say you are sorry for all that barking you did when we first arrived," said Jack. "Alright then," said the Alsatians. "We're sorry, so please let us in." "Ok." Jack opened the big gate and in they came, but this time they hung their heads in shame.

"Thanks Jack," one of them said. "We will never bark at you or Bea again." "You had better not," said Jack, feeling very superior. Jack and Bea ran on down the lane, past the sign post, then along by the river until they met Dal who was standing outside his house. They asked him to meet them at noon and bring all his friends to the wedding.

As they ran past he barked back to them,

"Alright, we will all meet you at noon." They told Boxer, and Boxer told all his friends. They told Tiger, and Tiger told all his friends, who in turn told all their friends. All the dogs in the neighbourhood were so excited to be invited to the biggest dog wedding there ever was.

Jack and Bea could hardly sleep that night, thinking about the next day, but they were so tired that, finally, they both fell asleep in each other's paws.

In the morning Bea woke with a start, looked outside at the big clock on the church spire nearby and shouted to Jack, "Jack, Jack. Get up it's almost nine o'clock and this is our wedding day. I have so much to do, I will never be ready on time." Jack got up, rubbed his eyes and took a long stretch.

"Don't fuss, we will make it in good time." Bea had a long bath. Jack got washed in the pond, playing with the resident ducks as he cleaned his paws. He would bark at them and try to catch one, but the ducks were always too quick for him.

"Stop playing around," he heard Bea bark. "Get yourself ready. We have a big day ahead of us." "Hope she is not going to start being a yap when

we get married," thought Jack. Jack gave himself a good shake and rolled a bit in the long grass. He shouted,

"That's me. I am ready to go." Bea came out to meet him. She was really beautiful. Her fur was very nicely combed, and she smelled of jasmine flowers, which she had rolled herself in after her bath. Jack told her how much he loved her, and they both set off to the Castle. As they were passing Tiger's house there were about twenty dogs waiting. As they passed the dogs all barked together,

"GOOD LUCK TO JACK AND BEA." Then they all started to follow the happy couple.

When they passed Boxer's house the same thing happened again, only this time there were forty dogs, and they ALL started to follow along the river path. Cats, mice, rats, all ran for cover when they saw all the dogs coming. At Dal's house there were another sixty dogs waiting, who joined in with the others on the way to the Castle.

This was surely going to be the biggest dog wedding in the whole county.

Shortly, they all arrived at the Castle. The

Alsatians opened the two large gates, stood behind them, and bowed their heads. One said, "Hi Jack and Bea." Jack gave them a quick bark back as he passed. The Alsatians could not believe their own eyes when they saw the crowd of dogs following to the wedding. There were over 100 guests. They had never seen so many dogs together in their life. There were small dogs, big dogs, spotty dogs, stripy dogs, and just plain black and white dogs.

Viking was also shocked to see how many were coming up the path. He was very pleased to see so many coming, because he just loved a good party. Viking called the head chef. "Look," he said, "Can you make enough food for this entire crowd?"

"Of course I can," said the chef. "There is plenty of meat and bones in the kitchen."

Viking told them all to go into the great hall. He asked Jack and Bea to wait at the front, while he showed all the rest to their seats.

When every dog was sitting quietly, Viking thanked them all for coming to the wedding on behalf of Jack and Bea. He then said, "Well, let's get these two married, so that the meal can be served." They all barked at once, "Good idea," for all dogs like their dinner, and no matter what, they did not want to wait too long.

"Jack," said Viking. "Do you love Bea?"

"Yes," said Jack.

"And Bea, do you love Jack?"

"Yes," Bea said very shyly.

"OK then. Will you both marry each other, and share all your bones in the future together? No matter how big and juicy they might be."

"Yes," barked Jack, "I WILL."

And, "I WILL ALSO," barked Bea.

"That's it then. I now pronounce you Dog and Bitch. You may now kiss the bride," he said to Jack. Jack gave Bea the biggest lick on the ear, and Bea did the same back to Jack, while all the 120 dogs barked and barked, "GOOD LUCK TO JACK AND BEA."

People could hear them for miles around and wondered what was happening.

The chef brought out the meat and the bones he

had prepared for dinner, and all the dogs ate as much as they could. They all sang songs, and told each other doggy tales well into the night.

JACK AND BEA HAVE PUPS

About two months had passed. Jack and Bea were very happy together. The other dogs in the neighbourhood were still talking about the big wedding, and all the fun they had that day, which lasted into the early hours of the next morning. The two Alsatians had become friendly with all the dogs, and instead of barking at them when they came near to the Castle, would let them in through the big gates to run in the grass. (Only when the Master was away of course.) As for Jack and Bea they could come any time to see Viking, who was now one of their best friends.

One morning Jack was in the usual pond getting his wash for the day, when he saw Bea coming up the garden path.

"OH Jack," she shouted, "I have some news for you."

"OH yes," said Jack, "and what could that be? You know I know everything that goes on around here, so how could it be new to me?"

"Well," said Bea, "This is new and I am the first to

know, and this time you are second."

"Huh," said Jack. "It had better be good. Tell me then."

"Well," said Bea, "Do you like children?"

"Yes, I suppose I do," said Jack.

"How would you like to be a dad?"

"I never thought about that!" said Jack.

"Well, wellllllll. You are going to be!!!" Jack was speechless.

"Me a DAD! My goodness," he said. Then again he said "ME A DAD!" louder than before. "What am I going to do? What am I going to wear? What am I going to say?" Bea stopped him right there. "You do not have to do anything. I am the one who has to have the pups, and all you have to do is help to feed and protect them until they grow up."

"I can do that OK," said Jack. "I can hunt. Remember the rabbit I caught when you were hungry?"

"Yes," said Bea, "You are a great hunter."

"And I will protect them. No other dog, or anyone,

will ever hurt them while I am about." "Yes of course," said Bea. "We all know you are very brave, so you have nothing to worry about. Just enjoy the pups when they come along and be a good Dad."

"I will," said Jack, now feeling very proud of himself for fathering some pups. "I must tell all the dogs."

"Not just yet please," said Bea. "It will be a few months yet before they are born. In fact it will be in winter."

"I can't wait," said Jack.

It was almost Christmas day when the pups were born. Luckily they were in a good warm shed. Richard had even put in a small electric heater for them. Jack watched as Bea counted the puppies after they were born. There were three, two girls and one boy. One of the girls was a little brown one, the other a white one and the boy was brown and white.

"What are we going to call them?" Bea asked. "How about Jas for the white one – because it looks a bit like me, and Bell for the brown one - because it looks a bit like you," said Jack.

"But the other brown and white one, what shall we call him?" asked Bea.

"I don't know," said Jack. "Let's wait until morning, and then we might think of a name for him."

The next morning Bea and Jack were up early. It was still very cold outside. They thought about how lucky they were to be in such a warm shed, and that Richard was very good to them. Bea was about to give the pups their breakfast when she noticed there was one missing.

"JACK, JACK, JACK," she shouted, "One is missing." Jack jumped off the straw he was sitting on, and started to look all around the shed. "He's not in here!" Jack barked. "He must have gone outside."

"OH! No not in this weather," said Bea anxiously.

"I will go out and look for him," Jack shouted. Jack looked all around the garden, he looked in the green house, he looked in the other sheds, he spoke to the hens, and then the ducks in the pond, but nobody had seen the other pup with no name.

"If only I had given him a name, I could have

shouted it, and he might have come to me." Jack was very sad, because he wanted to be the best Dad in the whole world, and yet he had lost his only son pup before it was a week old. Suddenly he heard a yelp. "Where did that come from?" Jack stood very still, and kept quiet. Again another yelp. This time he was able to trace the sound. It was coming from the rockery, at the very top of the garden. Jack ran up, and there among the snow and the rocks was the little pup, happily playing. Jack was so happy to find him, he forgot to scold him, and lifted him up by the neck to bring him back to the shed. Bea was so glad to see him she gave him lots of hugs and licks.

"I know now what I will call my son," said Jack.

"What?" asked Bea.

"I am going to call him ROCKY, because that's where I found him playing and he was happy. So ROCKY it will be."

Spring came and the pups had grown. Rocky was more adventurous than the others. He would have to look at everything; even if Richard set a bucket down in the yard Rocky would run to it, and give it a good sniff. He would go into all the sheds in the garden each day to see if there was anything different he could look at. Rocky was a clever pup, and he just wanted to know everything, like his dad did. One day Rocky was talking to Jack and Bea. He had heard about pedigree dogs and mongrel dogs, so he asked his parents what they were.

"Well said Jack, I am a pedigree Jack Russell, and your mum is a Pedigree Beagle."

"So what am I?" asked Rocky.

"Am I a mongrel?"

"Oh no," Jack and Bea barked together. "You must be a pedigree also." "But you two are different dogs, so I must be a mongrel. I must be!" Rocky said with a tear in his eye. He did not want to be a mongrel.

Jack thought quickly, "Of course you're not! You're a .... You're a ... hmm ....I mean you're a Pedigree Jackabee." "Yes" said Jack. "A pedigree Jackabee." Rocky jumped up and down, and then ran round in circles barking "I am a pedigree Jackabee." Rocky ran outside and told the hens, and the ducks - which really had no interest in what Rocky was; they just knew he was a dog and a lively one.

Rocky would chase the ducks and hens when they came out of the water, and they were getting a bit tired of it. As for the two girl pups they were very lady like; kept very much to themselves, and dreamed of having pups of their own some day.

Another three months passed. It was now summer and Rocky was getting bigger. He could almost run as fast as Jack. Rocky and his dad would also play fight in the garden. Jack knew his son was going to be strong, like him someday.

Bea came into the garden, "OK pups," she barked, "Its time you all had your injections. Richard is going to take you all to the vet's surgery tomorrow morning. It's only a little jab in your paw to keep you healthy, and afterwards he is going to buy you all a collar with your name on it. Isn't that wonderful?"

The girls liked the collar bit with the name tag. They thought it was like having a nice piece of jewellery, but they were a bit frightened of the jab. Rocky on the other hand was not frightened at all of the injection, but hated the thought of having to wear something that might look like jewellery, because he wanted to be like Jack, a really tough dog - not like a girl dog.

Don't forget he was a pedigree Jackabee, and proud of it.

TO THE VET'S

The next morning Richard was up bright and early. After breakfast he shouted to Jack and Bea, "Ok, Let's get these pups ready to go to the vets." Bea was fussing all over her pups, saying things like - "Now you be good Rocky, and you other two, don't be afraid. We all have had our injections at the vets; it's nothing to worry about."

Rocky thought, "It's not the injection, it's that silly collar I don't like." The two girls were being very brave, and saying, "Don't fret mum. We will be OK." Richard went to open the car door, "Now I want you all to be on your best behaviour at the vets." He looked at Rocky. "That means you too. No nonsense now."

Rocky was always up to something naughty. They all jumped into the back of the car, and off they went. The two girls were busy chatting in the back, and Rocky was looking out the side window at all the passing cars. Sometimes he would see another dog, and when he saw a cat he would growl and bark. Rocky really liked cats, because they would give him something to chase. He never caught one, because the cat could always run up a tree, or jump a fence which Rocky couldn't do. He would stand barking in frustration, and the cat would look at him from afar shouting - "Well, come on then, I'm waiting."

All of a sudden the car drew up beside a big house with lots of gardens.

"Was this the vet's surgery?" They all wondered together. The girls were not feeling so brave now, and if the truth were told, neither was Rocky. However, he kept up a very brave face in front of the others. Richard got out of the car and was reading a notice on the gate. It read that the vet had been called out on an urgent case, and would not be back again until 2pm - which was 2 hours from now.

Richard thought that rather than waste time, they would go and get the collars first. He drove on another mile or so, and stopped again. Richard told the dogs to wait until he came back with the collars, and to behave themselves. Again he looked straight at Rocky. Richard then went to the pet shop, and looked into the window. The dogs could see into the window too because the car was right along- side. They could see lots of different collars.

Some were pink, others were red and blue. There were large ones and small ones, thick ones and thin ones. Some had beautiful stars on them, which shone like diamonds. The girls were so excited, "Oh maybe we will get one like that; we could show it off to all our friends." Rocky was nearly sick at the thought of having to wear a pink collar with sparkling diamonds on it. He thought that every dog, cat, and even the birds would be laughing at him.

Richard suddenly came out of the shop with three parcels. When he got into the car - even before he had time to close the door, the girls wanted to see what they had been bought. Richard opened the first two parcels. They were the most beautiful pink and sparkling diamond collars, with their names on them. The girls were so pleased, they pressed their heads up to the window of the car so as any dogs passing would see them and be jealous. Rocky was horrified! He looked at his parcel and thought,

"If mine is the same as theirs I will surely die - right here and now." Richard opened the parcel for Rocky. His eyes opened wide, for there was the most "he man" dog collar he had ever seen! It was

all black with big silver studs, and a tag which said, "I am Rocky." He loved his collar, and let Richard put it on for him, while giving his hands big licks, to show how much he loved his master for buying such a sensible collar, fit for a tough dog like Rocky.

Richard had just finished putting on the collar when a big black cat walked passed the open door of the car. Rocky just could not help himself. He jumped straight out the door and almost landed on the cat's back. It hissed at Rocky and arched its back to scare him, but Rocky was having none of it. Rocky jumped at the cat, which turned and ran as fast as it could. Rocky chased it down the road. Richard was shouting, "Come back Rocky, Come Back!" at the top of his voice. Rocky heard nothing. All he could see was that big black cat, just in front of him. It turned into entries. It jumped over fences and into people's gardens. It ran into a field, over a river and then into a forest. Rocky was still following it. The cat was tiring, and so was Rocky.

The chase had been going on now for 30 minutes. Of course time did not matter to Rocky. He just wanted to catch that cat! Finally the cat ran up a tree. Rocky could not climb up so high. He stood at the bottom, tired and very cross.

"I will wait here - all night if I have to," he thought. "This cat will not get away."

ROCKY IS LOST

Meanwhile Richard was frantically looking for Rocky everywhere. "What am I going to tell Jack and Bea when I get home - Sorry I lost your pup? Jack will be very cross and Bea will be so sad. Oh, what am I going to tell them?"

Richard asked everyone he passed. "Please, have you seen a white and tan pup called Rocky?" Only one stranger said he had seen a dog, a bit bigger than a pup. It was tan, or brown and white, and it was chasing a cat at full speed.

"Where did it go please? What direction did it run?" asked Richard, with a little hope in his voice. "Well," said the man, "they both went into that forest on the hill."

"Ok," said Richard, "I will look there." Richard spent hours looking and calling for Rocky, but there was no sign of him. "It's getting dark now," thought Richard. I have to go back to get these other dogs home."

The car came in through the gate. Jack and Bea had been worried because the pups were very late getting home. "Hi," barked Jack. "Hi," barked Bea. "How did it go?" she asked the pups. "I hope you were not too frightened."

"Where is Rocky?" they both asked together. "I can explain," said Richard. "There's nothing to worry about. He is just lost for a bit; we will find him tomorrow. He is in the big forest, on the edge of town. You see I accidentally left the car door open for a second just as a big cat passed. Well you know how Rocky is when he sees a cat."

Jack answered saying, "You left the door open? Well, I suppose it's not too bad, now that he's been to the vet's for his injections. The vet will have put a microchip under his skin, with a number on it to identify him. When someone finds him they can hand him in. Isn't that right Richard?"

"Well, yes, it is right Jack, but, but, but I did not get to the vet. He was closed - some important job to do at the farm, so none of the dogs got their injections or chipped. I took them to get their collars with their names on."

"Yes," barked the girls. "Look at our lovely collars with our names and diamonds on them." Jack looked, but said nothing. He was furious with

Richard. Bea looked at the collars and said that they were very beautiful and looked lovely on the girls. Bea was also cross and very worried about Rocky. "Maybe some nice person will bring him into the town police station. So we will have to notify them and the town dog home first thing in the morning."

Rocky was still sitting under the tree looking up as the cat was looking down. He could hardly keep his eyes open. He suddenly fell asleep. The cat saw this, and sneaked down from the tree very quietly. He jumped over Rocky, and ran as fast as he could back home. Rocky woke. It was raining and for the time of year it was very cold. It was seven in the morning. The birds were beginning to make all sorts of weird sounds, to warn the other birds about Rocky being at the bottom of the tree. Rocky thought,

"What am I doing here?" Then he suddenly remembered that cat. He looked up - the cat had gone. He looked behind the tree. No cat there either.

"Oh well, that's another one that got away. I suppose I had better get home for my breakfast." Rocky had missed his lunch and his dinner and

was now very hungry. Rocky looked all around him. "Where am I? I can see nothing but trees. Which way should I go? I am really lost." Rocky was also getting a bit frightened now. He just wanted to get home to his mum and dad and have a good feed.

He saw a rabbit in the hedge. It was hopping along looking for breakfast too. Rocky thought he could catch it. He had heard his dad talk about catching rabbits and how good they were to eat. Rocky ran straight at the rabbit, which was indeed taken a bit by surprise. (Imagine a dog being so silly, that he did not know to crouch, and hide, then creep up slowly, if he wanted to catch a rabbit.) The rabbit simply took to his heels and ran off before Rocky could even get close. "Oh," said Rocky, "I am too slow, and have no experience of catching anything. I can't even catch a silly old cat. I will never be great, like my dad."

Rocky seemed to have been walking for miles when he came upon an old broken down farmhouse. There were some chickens outside, feeding in the grass. Rocky thought, "Now there is a feed. Surely I could catch a chicken." Rocky ran into the field beside the old farm house, and was just about to bite the neck of a really plump bird, when he heard a loud BANG. Rocky felt his legs go from beneath him, and he fell to the ground. "What has happened?" he yelled. Suddenly Rocky saw a big rough looking man coming towards him. "I missed you," he said. "I should have shot you dead – That's what I was trying to do - coming in here to steal my hens. I'll show you!" the man yelled at the top of his voice. He lifted up his gun and was about to shoot Rocky in the head, when his wife came out of the house.

"No, NO!" she shouted. "He can work for us. We will tie him up, and give him a few scraps now and then. He will help to keep the fox away at night; he will bark and we will know when Mr Fox is here."

"Good idea," said the man, who Rocky noted, was wearing big black boots. "You see these boots?" the man said to Rocky, Well, I will kick you with them if you don't tell us when that fox is about. Now we will tie you up near the hen house and there you will stay from now on!"

Months passed, and the bad man kept Rocky tied with a chain. He only fed him old scraps of meat and bones. Rocky was so sad.

Richard, Jack, Bea, and the girls now knew that they might never see Rocky again. Nobody had reported seeing him at the police station, or the dog home. Six months had now passed and Richard announced that he had been offered a new job in London, and was going to move the whole family there.

ROCKY ESCAPES

Once a week the bad old farmer and his wife would come out with the hose pipe to wash Rocky. The wife would stand and laugh as the old farmer, who was called Sam, would put the cold water hose on Rocky.

Poor Rocky would try to get away from the water, but because his chain was so tight he could not get very far. "Go on Sam. Do it again. Go on Sam, do it." Again and again the woman would shout to her husband.

"He's had enough." said Sam, Give him an old chicken bone for his dinner, and make sure there is no meat left on it. Can't be wasting good meat on a miserable mongrel like him."

Rocky was furious, but all he could do was cry to himself. "I wish I had never run after that cat. I wish I had stopped when I heard Richard calling me. I wish I could see my Mum and Dad again and my two sisters. I would never be bad again." He went on saying – "I wish, I wish this, and I wish that."

Night was falling. It was nearly winter, and Rocky was very cold. Then, all of a sudden he heard a strange voice coming from the bushes. It seemed to be saying the same thing as Rocky - "I wish, I wish."

"Who's there?" asked Rocky.

"It's me, and there is no point in going on saying "I wish, I wish." If you want to see your parents again, and get free of that chain, you have to do something. NOT just keeping on saying "I wish," because it will not happen by itself."

"Who are you?" asked Rocky.

"If you promise not to bark I will tell you, and I promise to be your friend."

"Well," said Rocky. I will not bark if you tell me now."

"OK, I am Fred."

"Fred?" said Rocky. "I do not know any dog called Fred."

"I am not a dog. Well, I suppose I am in a way, I am a dog's cousin."

"Are you saying you are my cousin?"

"Well, yes. I suppose I am" said the voice. "If you are not a dog, then what are you?"

"I am a fox."

"A FOX," Rocky shouted.

"Keep quiet Rocky. That mad and bad farmer will shoot me, and all my family, if you bark." "I won't" promised Rocky. "But my dad told me that foxes are not to be trusted; not one little bit. That's why people call you sly and crafty!"

"Of course we are crafty. We have to be. I have to live out here because nobody loves me, except one person I know, who loves all animals. I have to live on my wits or I would be dead long ago. Dogs want to chase and eat me. And people want to shoot me. Poor me, what did I ever do to anyone?"

"I don't know whether to trust you or not," said Rocky. "Maybe I will start to bark, and get you caught and maybe the old farmer will give me some more food for catching you."

"Maybe, Maybe, Maybe, and Maybe the moon IS made of cheese"

"Stop dreaming, and let me get you off that chain. That will prove to you that I am a friend you can

trust."

"How can you do that? Asked Rocky. Well a chain is only as strong as its weakest link, and so I will look for that link."

"OK," said Rocky, "If you can get me released I will not bark and I will trust you forever." Rocky looked into the hedge where the voice was coming from. He could see nothing. Then a pair of reddish, yellowish eyes appeared, followed by a huge head, and pure white teeth. Rocky had never seen anything like it before. As the big fox came closer, Rocky could see a red bushy tail, strong paws and hind legs. He was afraid in case the big fox was going to eat him.

"Let me see now," said Fred. He looked up and down the chain. "Hmmm, hmmmm," he muttered to himself. Finally he said, "Yes, there is one old link here and if we pull together we might break it." Rocky was so thankful. He had tried and tried to break the chain, but he was not strong enough.

"OK," said Fred, "Let me get my teeth on the chain, just behind your neck."

"OH!!" thought Rocky. "My dad was right. He is going to bite my head off." When Fred opened his

mouth, his teeth were 10 times the size of Rocky's. "Here goes, I am dead now," thought Rocky. The big Fox grabbed the chain and shouted "Pull, Pull, for all you're worth. Pull Rocky." Rocky pulled, and the big Fox pulled. They heard a creaking noise, and all of a sudden the two of them ended up rolling across the farmyard. Rocky's chain had broken, and he was free.

The big fox said "Right Rocky. Grab a chicken for dinner and follow me. I will teach you how to survive in a forest on your own. But meantime we will go to my den and you can meet the family. We have enough food now to feed everyone. You can tell us all about your time in the forest." "Are all foxes as friendly as you?" asked Rocky. "No way" said Fred, "I am not really all that friendly either. I needed to get you free from that chain, so as I can catch a chicken now and again. Remember I also have a family to look after." "So you are sly after all," said Rocky. "I suppose I am, but I did take a liking to you. I don't know why, but I did, I promise I will help you find your way." "I believe you," replied Rocky, but deep down he was not too sure if maybe HE was to be tomorrow night's dinner.

ROCKY IN THE FOXES DEN

Rocky followed Fred, each of them carrying a chicken through the forest over ditches and fields. They came to a big old oak tree, where Rocky could see a small hole going into its roots.

"This is home," said Fred. Then he shouted, "It's safe to come out you lot, the dog is my friend."

Fred's wife and young cubs peeked out.

"Hello," she said to Rocky.

"Hi there," Rocky said back.

"This is my wife Frances," said Fred, "And this is Rocky. We have a lot to tell you about our adventures today." Over dinner Rocky told them all about chasing a cat and getting lost in the forest, and how this awful man and his wife had kept him chained up for months.

"Yes we know," said Frances, "We have not had a good chicken since you were there. We were too frightened that you would bark and the farmer would shoot us. But here in the forest we have lots of food. There are many birds to catch, and there are plenty of rabbits, and by the stream we can

catch some fish if we are quick enough." "Oh," said Rocky "I wish I could learn to do all that. My dad could, but now I am lost and he is not around to teach me. I need to learn to defend myself and to catch food."

"Yes you do," said Fred, "and you need to know how to keep warm and how not let people catch you, or goodness knows what will happen next time. Tomorrow we will start. We will teach you. So up early, as soon as the crows start singing, if you could call it that."

"More like squawking!" said Mrs Fox, with a funny laugh.

Rocky slept well that night, he was well fed and toasty warm in the den.

He looked outside. Fred was already awake and getting ready to hunt for breakfast. "Let's go Rocky. Just you watch how it's done. Fancy a nice tasty crow? They make a great breakfast." Rocky watched as Fred slowly walked into a nearby field, which was full of cows. "Now be very quiet," he said, "We do not want to disturb the cows because that would give the game away." Rocky stood very still and watched as Fred rolled himself in some cow dung. He smelt terrible. Fred whispered to Rocky - "Now you do the same!" "Yuck, how awful," he thought but he did as he was told.

"Now do you see those crows feeding over there?"

"Yes," said Rocky.

"Well I want you to sneak under the hedge until you get close to them without making a noise. I will sneak up the other hedge and we will surround them. When I howl we both run towards them, and in their confusion we should be able to grab a couple each."

Rocky got into position. He waited ever so quietly. The crows were busy picking up the little insects that the farmer had uncovered when he had cut the grass the day before. Suddenly Rocky heard this loud howling noise, like a "woo, woo, woo." It even scared Rocky - never mind the birds.

Rocky could see Fred running straight at the birds, which were trying to fly away, but were actually heading straight towards Rocky. Rocky ran out from the hedge and so the crows did not know what way to turn. Grab, Snap, Grab. The big fox had caught three of them. Rocky jumped as high as he could. Grab, yes he caught one! He pulled it to the ground and quickly snapped its neck with his jaws.

"Well done, well done," shouted Fred.

Rocky thought to himself, "If only my dad could see me now he would be ever so proud of me." They brought back the four crows. Mrs Fox had the fire going and they all had a great breakfast.

"I will show you more later. How would you fancy a nice tasty rabbit for tea, or maybe some trout?" asked Fred.

"Rabbit sounds good to me," Rocky said, lying back contentedly, after his feed of crow.

Later that evening, off they went again, and Rocky caught his first rabbit. Then he learned to fish, and to look after himself in the forest over the next few months. Rocky loved being with the foxes, and played with the young ones when they were not hunting. It was now nearly spring and Fred was telling Rocky that this was a bad time of year for foxes.

"Why is that?" Asked Rocky.

"Well it seems that people don't like us on their

land. They gather together lots of dogs and horses and then they make a terrible noise, with something that they put into their mouths. It can be very frightening! Then they chase us through the fields until we collapse with exhaustion. The big dogs, called hounds, catch us and rip us into tiny pieces."

"I don't believe it! That's just terrible," said Rocky. "Really terrible! I will protect you."

"I know you would Rocky but there can be at least fifty hounds after one little fox. He has no chance. Anyway let's not think about that, let's go over to that bad old farmer and get some of HIS chickens for tonight's dinner."

"Great," said Rocky,

"I WOULD LIKE TO GET EVEN WITH THAT FARMER."

ROCKY SAVES THE FOXES

It was early the next morning when Fred and Rocky set out to the old Farmer's field where he kept the chicken hut. They crossed over the ditches and fields full of wheat. They kept close to the hedgerows so as not to be spotted by anyone. Rocky had learned to roll in cow's dung to hide his scent from would be predators or any prey he had in mind to catch. He now knew how to think like a fox, craftily and cunningly. He had learned to run as fast as any other animal. He had learned to survive on his own. Soon they were almost at the hen hut. Fred stopped.

"Look," he said to Rocky. "Look there, beside the door of the house." Rocky looked to where Fred pointed, and there sitting beside the door was the big gun. "I am feeling a bit worried," said Fred.

But Rocky thought "This is my chance to get even." He told Fred not to be scared, "I have a great idea. Let's push the gun round to the side of the hen hut. I know there is a very long drop and a deep river there. We could push the gun into it."

"That way it would be gone forever," said Fred.

"Yes," said Rocky," "and you could have a chicken or two anytime you wanted."

"Great idea Rocky, let's try." The two of them very quietly sneaked behind the hen hut. They did not want to frighten the hens in case they made a lot of noise and woke the farmer. They came to the big gun. Rocky pushed it over until it was lying on the ground. Fred got his big teeth into the wooden butt of the gun and Rocky got the barrel end. Together they were able to move it across the yard, behind the hen hut and over to the deep river.

"Right one last push and over it goes," said Rocky. They gave it a last big shove. It fell over, and on the way down it hit a large rock. The gun fired, BANG, then again BANG.

It was to be it's last shot. It fell into the river and went straight to the bottom. The farmer and his wife heard the two loud bangs, and ran outside as quickly as they could - in their nightgowns. Rocky and Fred were watching, and started to laugh at the pair of them running about in their nightwear, not knowing what to do without their gun. Rocky shouted to them, "I think we will have a chicken or two now for dinner, and there is nothing you can do about it." Fred and Rocky grabbed a couple each and walked off down the path. The bad old farmer and his wife were furious, but could do nothing about it. They turned to go back into the house when a stream of water came running at them from out the front door.

Rocky, unknown even to Fred, had slipped round the back and put the hose pipe that they had always used on him, through the back door, and turned it up full. The house was a mess, and the chickens were running everywhere, because the back gate had been left open.

"That will teach those two horrible people a lesson," Fred said. "Yes indeed you are as smart as a fox, and not to be messed with."

It was eleven o'clock, and a beautiful bright spring morning. The sun was shining, but without being too hot. The two were feeling very happy with themselves as they crossed the fields with the chickens, back to the den. Suddenly Rocky heard a strange noise in the distance.

"Did you hear that noise?" Rocky asked Fred.

"I heard something, and I hope it is not what I

think it is." The noise sounded again, it was closer this time. Fred dropped the chickens and shouted, "Run, run for your life. It's the hounds," Rocky did as he was told and dropped the chickens before running as fast as he could after Fred. Rocky could see that Fred was really scared. He had never seen him run so fast. Rocky was quick, but could hardly keep up with him.

Rocky looked back. There, coming over the mound in the last field were at least one hundred hounds, all barking and showing their teeth. Behind them came about one hundred men on horses, making loud and strange sounds. They were whipping their horses and shouting, "Faster, faster." Rocky had never seen anything like it. He was also very frightened. Fred was running towards his den. He thought that would be the safest place, because the den had many other exits through the forest. The hounds were big, with long legs, and were getting closer and closer all the time.

Finally when the two made it into the den the hounds were only seconds away. They were too large to get in, but were waiting outside. With the hounds barking and howling and the men blowing their horns, and the horses snorting, the noise was very frightening for all the family. The hounds surrounded the den, at every exit. There was no escape for the family. They were doomed.

"What are we going to do?" asked Rocky.

"We can do nothing, said Fred, Soon the hounds will claw their way into the den and tear all of us into tiny pieces."

"Not if I can help it" said Rocky, "I have an idea --- See you all sometime!!"

"Rocky, Rocky, Please do not go out there." Rocky ran to the exit and out into the forest. The hounds were taken by surprise at this cheeky and brave little fox coming out. Rocky ran for all he was worth. The hounds followed him, and so did the men and the horses. He ran and ran through fields and ditches until he was about three miles away from the den. Then he sat down. The hounds surrounded him barking and growling. The lead hound shouted, "Hey wait a minute that is not a fox. It's a dog, like us."

"Yes," said Rocky, "I think you all need glasses, chasing me like that!!! I think I will report you to the dog council."

"Who?" asked the boss dog.

"Have you never heard of the dog council?" Rocky barked.

"No I have not."

"Well," said Rocky. "If I tell them how you chased me you will all be banned from hunting from now on. Your masters will not like that! You will be put into dog homes. And another thing - leave the foxes alone in this part of the forest in future - or I will report your mistake."

"Oh please don't," said the boss hound. "We will not chase them anymore."

"Ok then," said Rocky, "So just watch out." Rocky laughed into himself because he knew that there was no such thing as a dog council. He was just being as crafty as the foxes had taught him to be.

ROCKY MEETS THE LORD OF THE MANOR

Soon the horses and the riders arrived on the scene. "What's this? A dog out here in the forest. What are you doing here Dog?" demanded a big man with a red coat and a top hat. Rocky thought he looked very silly riding a horse with a top hat.

"I am lost Sir," Rocky replied.

"What's your name?" he demanded in a loud voice. Rocky did not like him.

"It's Rocky - I am a pedigree Jackabee."

"You're a what?" laughed the man. "A pedigree what?"

"I am a pedigree Jackabee. My father is a pedigree Jack Russell and my mum is a pedigree Beadle, so therefore I am a PEDIGREE JACKABEE!" Rocky shouted at the man, beginning to get a little angry.

"Well, whatever you are, you should not be here in this forest alone. You will come with us back to the

Manor and meet his lordship. He might let you stay for a few days." A couple of hours later Rocky was going in through a grand gateway towards a very large house. All the dogs followed, this time behind the horses, in rows of twos, like soldiers on parade. They were all very well trained and ever so well behaved. The big hounds lined up first at the feeding bowls, then came the smaller ones. They all ate in turn, in a very orderly fashion.

Rocky looked on, thinking that these dogs were not at all like the foxes in the den, where each one eat their food as fast as possible, with no manners at all. Rocky was given a bowl of dog nuts. "Yuck!" he thought. "Nothing like the taste of a good fresh chicken or rabbit."

After dinner Rocky was brought to meet the Lord of the manor.

"Well young Rocky, I hear you have been lost in the woods. You had better be careful in case you get caught by those rough, bad foxes out there. They would eat a little dog like you in no time. Rocky thought to himself that these people didn't understand the foxes. They also had to eat, and if left alone, everyone could live together in peace.

Rocky said, "Yes sir, I know what you mean Sir," not wanting to offend the Lord of the Manor.

"So, I am told you are a pedigree Jackabee. I have never heard of a Jackabee dog before."

"Well," said Rocky "You have now and I am sure there are many things in this world that you have not heard tell of."

The Lord looked at him.

"You are a cheeky little Jackabee aren't you?"

"I am not cheeky, but I can look after myself, and stand up for myself, because I was taught by the fo--." He nearly said foxes and he knew that this would displease everyone. They must never find out that he was friends with the foxes. So he said "Taught by Fred. I was going to say, he is a good friend of mine." Naturally everyone thought that Fred was just another doggie friend of Rocky's.

"Well you can stay for a few days, but after that we will have to take you to the dog pound in the town. You have a collar and a name tag, so you must belong to somebody."

"I do," said Rocky. "I belong to my mum and dad, and I have two sisters. We all stay in a big house

on the edge of town, with Richard, who is our owner."

"Right," said the Lord of the Manor, "You can now go and take a rest. I will have a carriage ready in the morning to bring us to town."

The next morning the carriage was ready and waiting. Breakfast was served. Not again! More dog nuts! Rocky thought that these hounds did not know how to enjoy life, or what good food they were missing. A nice pigeon, a tasty blackbird, or maybe even a crow - (if there was nothing else about) would be a lot better than these awful nuts - day in and day out, for breakfast, dinner, and tea. The Lord and two of his servants got into the carriage, while another was sitting on top, holding the reins of two magnificent horses. Rocky was told to get into the holding pouch, at the back of the carriage. That was where the luggage was stored.

Off they went towards the town. About two hours passed, and Rocky began to recognize some of the houses and lamp posts as they got closer to the town. Suddenly Rocky shouted, "Stop! Stop! This is where I live with Richard and all my family." The Lord stopped the carriage and Rocky jumped down from the holding pouch and ran up the garden path.

"I am home, I am home!" he shouted. But instead of meeting Jack and Bea, a huge black Bull Dog came out barking, telling Rocky to clear off.

"This is my house now. You do not live here anymore."

Rocky was so sad he began to cry. The big bull dog felt a little bit sorry for Rocky, and told him that Richard and all the family had gone to live in London, many months ago. He said, "they had looked everywhere for you, but could not find you, so they were forced to leave as they had to go to London." By this time his lordship had come up the path.

"So sorry," he said to Rocky. "You will have to go to the dog pound until somebody gives you a home. I am sorry I can't look after you myself, but you know how many dogs I have already, and you just would not fit in with them."

Rocky was willing to accept his fate. He did not want to be a stray dog. He wanted to have a home of his own, and to be loved by some kind person. He would give them lots of love back.

ROCKY IN THE DOG POUND

Rocky was brought to the dog pound in the town centre. The man in charged looked at him. "That's a right scruffy dog you have there Sir. Where did you find him?"

"He was lost in the forest," said the Lord.

"Is that so? I see he has a name tag."

"Yes," said the Lord. "His name is Rocky and he says he is a pedigree."

"He's the funniest looking pedigree I have ever seen!" said the man in charge of the dog pound.

"Don't worry your Lordship we will keep him for ten days and then it will be the chop, chop." Rocky wondered what chop, chop meant. Maybe he was going to get nice meaty chops for dinner, if he stayed for ten days or more. Rocky thought that he could get to like this place.

He was taken by the man down a long corridor which smelt of disinfectant. It made Rocky feel a bit sick. He could hear other dogs barking in the distance, but they were not happy barks; they were barks of distress, worry and depression. Rocky began to get a bit worried himself. Maybe this place was not too nice after all. He was put into a cage which had a hole at the far end. Rocky looked through the hole. It led to a patch of gravel and bits of worn grass. Rocky went through the opening. From outside he could see many other dogs. They were all looking very sorry for themselves.

"Who are you?" one of them asked. "When did you get to this place?" another one asked. "Does nobody want you either?" said a small dog, hiding in the corner.

"I am Rocky; I arrived here today, and yes, my owner does want me, but I got lost in the forest, and a kind man brought me here to find him." "There are no kind people in here," said an old dog that had come up to hear what was going on.

"I heard the man at the desk say that I would be getting some chops in ten days! I think that's kind," said Rocky. The dogs looked at Rocky, and all began to laugh.

"You are silly. What he meant was that if someone

does not claim you from here in ten days time you will be taken through the black door at the bottom of the hallway, and from there no dog EVER comes back.

"You mean.....,?"

"Yes," said the big old dog, "We do mean, Chop. I have been here for nine days now and so tomorrow is my last. I may as well say goodbye to you all now." With a tear in his eye he went back to where he was lying.

Rocky thought, "This is no good. I will have to get out of here, but how? The place is like a jail, bars everywhere, cages, and barbed wire netting surrounding the outside." Next morning the warden came in early, and threw in a few slops for breakfast.

"Am I supposed to eat this?" asked Rocky.

"Do what you want," said the man. "I am going to have my bacon and eggs now. Good luck! And by the way, you had better try to look a bit tidier. There are people coming today looking for a dog to take home."

Some of the dogs ran into the wash room and gave

themselves a quick shower. Rocky did the same, and tidied himself up a bit. Later that day two people were walking around looking at all the dogs. Rocky could hear them saying "This one's nice." "No, I don't like It's markings. What about that one? It looks like a good dog. Or what about that little white and tan one over there, he looks nice." They were looking at Rocky.

"No way," said the other person. "He's too small; we want a good strong dog to guard our house." Rocky barked and barked as loud as he could, to show these people he that he could be a really good guard dog. But it was too late. They had picked an Alsatian, and were on their way out with him. The next day more people came, and went. This continued for another nine days, but nobody picked Rocky, no matter how much he tried to be as nice, or as tough as he thought the people might want him to be. It was now day ten and the warden told Rocky that he would be coming to give him the chop right after dinner!!

"You can have a special dinner today Rocky, as it will be your last," he said laughing. Rocky was very sad. "Why does nobody love me or want me?" he-cried.

"I want you," said a voice. Rocky looked up. There was a woman standing looking at him. "I run a dog's home called Benvarden. It's on the very North Coast of Ireland, and I take in young healthy dogs until I can find a home for them. I never give up trying to help a lost dog. Sometimes we even get real chops to eat!" Rocky could hardly believe his luck.

"Thank you! Thank you so much. I will be ever so good, and never give you any trouble."

"Right," said the woman, "That's it then. I will see the warden, and get you out of this place straight away. We have a long journey ahead of us."

ROCKY GOES TO BENVARDEN

The nice lady, who was called Louise, brought Rocky to the desk at reception. "Now you wait there until I fill in all the forms to get you released."

"OK," said Rocky, "But can I please use the dog toilet?"

"Of course you can," said Louise. "Now run along, but don't be away too long!"

Rocky ran down the big corridor to where all the other dogs were kept. "Listen boys," he said, "I do not have much time, so you must all be quick." Rocky opened all the cage doors by pulling back the lock with his teeth.

"Now run for all your worth. There is a hole in the fence which I made just in case I would not be picked to get out of here. I was not going to be chopped! When you get through the hole run towards the forest, and look out for a big fox called FRED. He will help you stay free."

Rocky watched as all the dogs dashed through the

hole in the fence, and then he ran back to the reception area.

"Ah Rocky, Just in time. We are finished and ready to go."

"Great," said Rocky.

The nasty warden said, "Well, good bye. I am going to check on these other dogs now."

Rocky jumped into the van Louise was driving, and looked out of the back window. After a minute or two, as they were driving away, he could see the warden coming out of the front door, shouting and waving his fists in the air.

"You did this Rocky. I just know you did!" Rocky laughed and said nothing.

The journey took around four hours, as they had to travel 120 miles to Benvarden. Rocky slept most of the way, on a big rug inside the van. At last he heard Louise calling to him,

"Wake up Rocky, we have arrived." The back doors opened, and a kind looking man called John was standing outside.

"Come on Rocky. Come with me, and I will show

you to the kennel you will share with the other dogs." Rocky followed, and Louise came up behind the two of them.

Rocky was shown into the kennel area. There were about thirty other dogs, all chattering to each other. "This is Rocky," Louise announced in a loud voice. All the dogs stopped chatting and looked at Rocky.

"Hi Rocky," they all said at once. All except a beautiful tan colored bitch with a white spot on her nose. The beagle was about the same age at Rocky. She thought to herself, "He is so handsome and rugged I will have to get to know him a little better." Her name was Betsy, and over the next few days she made sure to meet Rocky in the play yard at every opportunity. She would come up very close, so that Rocky could smell her nice scent and notice her.

"Hello," Rocky said, "What is your name?"

"It's Betsy," the Beagle said shyly, although she was not at all shy. "And what's yours?" She already knew since the first day he came in, but wanted to pretend that she had no interest in him.

"It's Rocky."

"That's a really tough dog's name, and I love your collar with all the silver studs."

"How long have you been here?" asked Rocky.

"Just about one week. There have not been too many people looking for dogs lately. One big male called Al got a home last week. People seem to be looking for big guard dogs, not little dogs like you and me."

"I am as good a guard dog as any, and as tough as those big dogs! I was trained by foxes you know."

"Oh, I thought foxes were dangerous, because of their big teeth and claws." "They are, but I soon showed them who was boss!" said Rocky, starting to show off to impress Betsy. He did not really need to, as she had fallen for him the minute she had seen him, and even wanted to marry him someday! Over the next few days a few people came and went.

Some took a dog, others went away without. Rocky and Betsy were becoming great friends. Each day they would play and chat together. Rocky would tell her stories about the forest, and how he had learned so much from the foxes. He told her all about Richard, and how he got lost chasing a cat. Then there was the time he was caught by the bad farmer, and how Fred and he had caught the chickens. "Ah," said Rocky. "Sometimes I miss those days. I still call them the good old days."

"Don't be sad," said Betsy "You are still young. You will have many more adventures - and maybe we will have some together." Rocky looked at her, not too sure what to make of that last comment.

Two more days passed. Rocky liked being at Benvarden. He thought Louise was very good to all the dogs, as she petted and groomed each one in turn. Also there was real meat to eat - not those dried up nuts which the Lord of the Manor fed to his hounds.

He went into the play yard and was shocked when he saw what was happening. Two people had picked Betsy to take home with them. Betsy looked at Rocky with a tear running down her face, as if to say, "I will never see you again." Rocky tried to cheer her up saying, "Come on now Betsy. Be happy. You are getting a home at last. We will meet again. I will always love you."

That cheered Betsy up a lot and she smiled. The

two people, who looked very nice and kind, took Betsy on a lead to their car. Rocky cried as he watched the car drive away from the yard. Betsy looked out the back window until Benvarden was no longer in sight.

ROCKY GETS A HOME

Rocky was very moody for the next few days. Even when people came to see him and were interested in taking him home, he growled at them, and of course the people went away thinking that he was a cross dog. They wouldn't want him about their house. Rocky didn't care. He just wanted Betsy back to himself. Louise came to speak to him.

"You will never get a home if you carry on like that. Nobody will want you. You will have to be nice and remember you will never meet Betsy again in here. At least if you are with some other people outside you might meet her again." "Where did they take her?" asked Rocky.

"Those nice people live in a town called Port Stewart - not too far from here. So, cheer up Rocky. If you do not meet Betsy again there are many other fish in the sea." Rocky wondered what Louise meant, fish in the sea? "I don't want a fish I want my Betsy."

Later that day two people came in looking for a good strong dog to take for walks. They looked at

Rocky, who growled at them, because he forgot what Louise had said. Rocky saw the couple walk away and look at other dogs in the pound. He thought to himself, "Louise is right; I will never get out of here if I do not behave nicely. When I do get out I will run away and maybe find the forest and the foxes again. But, I am now more than a hundred miles away from that forest. I could never find it again."

Rocky was now on his best behavior. The two people came back again to see him. "Are you a good dog?" One of them asked. Rocky was about to bark, but instead licked her hand through the cage. "I like this dog," Rocky heard her say to her husband.

"Yes he looks OK. Get Louise to put him on a lead and we will take him a walk."

Louise put Rocky on a lead and whispered to him, "You be good and don't pull or misbehave. You never know, you might get a home." The couple walked Rocky round the field, and agreed to take him home. Rocky was delighted that he was getting out, and he quite liked the couple too. After all the paper work was finished Rocky jumped into the waiting car and off they went. He sat up on the lady's knee and looked out the front window. Rocky watched everything that passed, cars, motorbikes, buses, people, and especially dogs because he was trying to see if he could see Betsy.

It was not long until the car stopped. This looked like a strange place he was going to live in. First they had to go through a barrier and then they turned onto a tiny road. Rocky heard the man say, "Well, here we are back at the Caravan."

"So I am to live in a Caravan," thought Rocky. "This is nice and comfortable," he noticed when he went inside.

"Well Rocky," said the man, "I am Mal and this is Mue". Rocky thought those were funny names. He looked around and found some food in a dish. Rocky ate all that was on offer and after a good sniff all around the Caravan he realized he was tired after all the events of the day. Rocky curled up on the sofa and fell asleep.

He slept well until the next morning. He had sausages for breakfast.

"This is alright here," he thought, "I will give it a few more days before I run away."

After breakfast Mal asked Rocky if he would like to run on the beach for a while. Rocky just stared back at him, "A beach!" he thought. "What is a beach? I have never heard of such a place."

"Well let's go," said Mal, "I will bring a ball and you can chase it." They walked through the Caravan Park, past the barrier and down the road. Rocky could smell something he never smelt before. He wondered what this could be. Then they reached the beach. Lots of other dogs were running and chasing balls, some were play fighting, other older dogs were just walking along beside their owners, thinking how unruly the youth of today were. "In our day we walked beside our masters and did as we were told."

Rocky was allowed to run free on the beach. He ran and ran and jumped into the air. Soon he started to dig holes in the sand. He was so happy.

Then he saw the sea.

"What is that?" Rocky wondered and ran closer to it. He was very careful and put his paw in first, pulling it out again very quickly, as the sea was very cold. He ventured in a little further and felt the water tickle his tummy, which felt nice. Then a

big wave suddenly covered him. It scared him a bit and he ran out - back onto the dry sand. Rocky gave himself a good shake down to get the water off, and then started to chase the ball that Mal had thrown for him. What a day! It was the best he had ever had, and Rocky dreamed about the beach all night.

Morning came and Rocky had more sausages with some egg and little bits of bacon for breakfast. He thought "Maybe I will not run away. This is too good to be true. I really like it here and these two with the funny names are very good to me." He went to the beach again that morning, and then Mue took him to the forest nearby. Rocky loved the fact that he could get all the same smells as he did when he was in the first forest. He could smell rabbits, and birds, as well as some smaller animals like hedgehogs and rodents living in the fields.

After a week of being in the Caravan Rocky heard Mal saying to Mue, "It's time to go home, we will have to pack up and go soon."

"What do they mean home? I thought this was home," said Rocky to himself. All the clothes and bits and pieces were put into the car and Rocky got

in too, of course in his usual place, on Mue's knee in the front seat. He heard Mue saying, "We will be in Whitehead in one and a half hours."

"Whitehead, where is that or what is that?" Rocky thought to himself.

The time passed and Rocky peered out of the window watching every dog pass.

Soon he fell asleep on Mue's knee.

ROCKY DISCOVERS WHITEHEAD

Rocky felt the car stopping. He looked out of the window but couldn't see very much; just some houses and steps. Mue put the lead on Rocky and took him up the steps.

"Wow!" he thought. "I can see lots from here, and there is the sea. I thought we had gone a lot further than this." (Rocky didn't realize that this was another part of the sea, and that the sea was enormous.)

He went into the house. "This is a lot bigger than the caravan," he said to himself. "Lots of places to hide bones and things." He sniffed everywhere. First, all around the downstairs, then up each stair and into each bedroom. He sniffed everything very carefully. He thought that he liked it here also, and hoped he would get more sausages for breakfast.

Rocky was a bit fussy about his food now days and would only eat Cookstown pork sausages because he thought they were the best. Mue had bought some for him before she left the Caravan Park in Castlerock. Rocky watched as Mal and Mue brought all the luggage up the steps. Mue told him she would take him for a walk after that long journey. She put him on the lead and walked down Cable Road towards the sea.

Rocky stopped at every gateway to sniff new scents. He saw a cat standing in one of the driveways, and much as he tried not to chase it, he did anyway! He remembered the trouble it had brought him the last time, but the fun was too much for Rocky. He just could not help it. Rocky took a dive at the cat but he had forgotten he was on a lead. The extending lead went out full length and poor Mue was nearly pulled off her feet. Rocky was very strong and fast even though he was just over a year old.

When they got to the path called Blackhead which led all the way to the lighthouse, Mue let Rocky off the lead so that he could exercise himself and run as fast as he wanted to. Rocky saw lots of seagulls and other birds on the stony beach at Whitehead. There was little sand, not like Castlerock where there were miles of beautiful beaches covered in thick golden sand. However Rocky enjoyed climbing over the rocks, jumping from one to another without getting his feet wet .This was a game he invented for himself. Rocky rounded a corner on the path where he could see an open field, and at the top of the field he could see three rabbits running and playing in the sunshine. "I want to play too," he thought, and made a dash for the hole in the fence. He ran straight to the rabbits, forgetting everything the foxes had taught him. Of course the rabbits saw him and ran away. Rocky gave chase; he ran after the three of them, but the rabbits split up and ran in different directions.

Rocky got confused as to which one he should chase. The rabbits ran into their burrows and waited for Rocky to pass by. One cheeky rabbit popped out of its burrow and shouted to Rocky, "Hi slow coach, maybe next time you'll be quicker!" Rocky did not think this was very funny and thought that they would be sorry next time, because he would sneak up, like the foxes taught him to catch them. Rocky loved playing on the rocks. He found small crabs in the pools between the rocks and loved eating them raw. (OK for dogs but not for humans, unless well cooked.)

He found lots of tasty seaweed to chew on, and lots of other dogs to play with. Rocky followed another large dog that jumped into the sea from a high rock. This was the first time Rocky was in deep water and had to swim to shore. He found the experience lots of fun and did it again and again, learning to swim further and further each time, even against the tide. Because Rocky ate all his dinners it made him really strong.

Two days passed and this time Mal took Rocky along the path at the shore. Soon they came to the big field where the rabbits where. Sure enough there they were, running and dancing at the far end. Rocky saw the cheeky one, and thought he would teach him a lesson. Rocky slipped into the hedge at the side of the field. Mal was chatting with some friends and did not see what Rocky was doing.

Rocky first rolled in some cow's dung and then slowly crept under the hedge. He was now only a few metres from the rabbit. He could hear the rabbit being cheeky to his friends, saying things like, "I'm the best runner, I'm the best fighter, I'm the best at everything!" Rocky took one dive and landed right on top of the cheeky little rabbit. The rabbit almost fainted.

"Who's the best now?" asked Rocky. "Your friends all got away, they must be better than you."

"Oh, Oh, please, please," squealed the Rabbit "I am sorry I gave you so much cheek. Please don't eat me." Rocky showed his teeth. The rabbit closed his eyes and waited for the big bite. Rocky told him that this must be his lucky day, because he had had his sausages this morning and was not hungry. Otherwise the rabbit would be his breakfast. The little rabbit thanked him so many times that Rocky had to tell him to be quiet.

Satisfied that the rabbit had learned a lesson, Rocky told him to go over to all the Rabbits and explain that he had been rude, and would never be cheeky again. Rocky then told him, "If I come into this field again I want a good run and chase, so maybe we could all be friends and have some fun together. I promise not to bite any of you." The rabbit started again, "Thank you, thank you, thank you ..."

"Enough of that," Rocky said. "Run along now and tell your friends what I said."

ROCKY SAVES THE CHILDREN

About a week later Rocky was playing with the Rabbits in the field, when he heard some people shouting, "Help! Help!" Rocky ran down the field to see what was happening. There was a crowd gathering on the rocks at the shore. Rocky heard one man saying, "They will surely drown. Stupid kids going out in a rubber dingy in weather like this. They will be half way to Scotland soon." Actually the weather was not too bad, but the tide was on the way out and there was a wind gathering.

"Has anybody called the life boat yet?" the man asked.

"Yes we have but it is attending another rescue, we will have to wait until it is free again, and that could be hours!!" another man said.

"And look, the dingy is leaking water. It's slowly beginning to sink.

"Are there any good swimmers?" another person asked the crowd. Each one looked at the other and shook their heads. Nobody there could swim so far

out to sea in such cold water. And try to get back again against the tide would be impossible.

"I am afraid these kids are doomed!" Rocky was listening to all this, and thought to himself that he would try. He just couldn't let these kids drown. Rocky climbed to the highest rock close to the water's edge. He jumped as far as he could into the sea.

The crowd was amazed.

"Look" one shouted, there is a dog in the water and its heading for the dingy. Rocky had noticed there was rope hanging from the dingy normally used for tying behind a yacht as a safety boat. The kids were still shouting "Help! Help!" But they were too far from shore now for anybody to hear them.

Rocky was swimming for all he was worth towards the dingy. He was nearly out of breath when he reached the rope. The two boys looked very scared indeed. Rocky gave them a little bark, just to say he was here to help them. He grabbed the rope in his teeth and pulled as hard as he could. Slowly, but very slowly the dingy began to turn and head back to the shore. Rocky was swimming against the tide and pulling the dingy behind him, and now the wind was getting stronger and stronger.

"I will never make it," thought Rocky, "It's just too much and too heavy for me."

He kept going as best as he could; his heart was pounding; he was swallowing some water. Rocky could just about see the people on the shore. They were a long way off. He pulled and pulled and was almost forced to give up when he heard a strange whirling noise above his head. Rocky was scared; he had never had heard anything like it before. He looked up, and there was a big helicopter, with RESCUE in red letters written on the bottom of it.

"We're saved!" thought Rocky. The men in the helicopter lowered a ladder and one of them climbed down into the dingy.

"Well done Rocky," he said. "If it had not been for you these kids would be in the middle of the ocean by now. Well done." He helped the two boys up the swinging ladder and then gave them a good scolding for going out in a dingy without an adult. They lifted Rocky into the helicopter too and let him sit beside the pilot. Rocky loved looking down at everyone below, they all looked so small. The

helicopter had to land at its own base in Hollywood. This was an Army camp near Bangor on the other side of Belfast Lough from Whitehead. Rocky wondered how he was going to get home from here.

"Don't worry Rocky," said the pilot, "we have a special car for you." Just then a police car pulled up beside Rocky and the pilot.

"Jump in and we will take you home. You are a hero now Rocky for saving those boys lives. Your picture will be in all the papers tomorrow, wait until you see." The police car sped off down the road with its lights flashing and its sirens blaring. Rocky sat in the front seat as usual. He was amused to see all the other traffic on the road pulling into the side to let them passed. Soon he was back in Whitehead and everyone had come out onto the footpaths to greet him, shouting, "Good dog Rocky, brave Rocky. You are a hero Rocky." Rocky was a bit embarrassed with all the attention he was getting and just wanted to have a good feed and a long sleep.

ROCKY GETS A SURPRISE

Rocky woke with a jolt. Someone was knocking at the door and he could hear a dog barking. "I know that bark," thought Rocky, It sounds like my dad's bark - but how could it be?" Mue opened the door and asked the tall man what he wanted. "You don't know me," said the man, "but I saw Rocky's picture in the newspaper and wanted to meet him."

"That's fine," said Mue, "Come on in, I'll see if he is awake yet. You know he was very tired after his swim and all the drama yesterday." Rocky was listening in the other room. "Yesterday!" he said to himself, "I must have slept all night and yet I thought I was only asleep for a few hours. Oh I must have been really tired."

Rocky came into the room where the man was standing. He stared at him and then with a bark of delight he jumped into his arms. He knew it was Richard; and with him was Jack, Rocky's dad. Rocky had a thousand questions which he wanted answered all at once. "Where did you go? I found the house but you were not there. How are my mum, and my sisters? Where do you all live now?" Rocky went on and on.

"Hold on." said Richard, "WE have some questions first. "Where did you get to after you jumped out of the car? And how did you get here? And who are these nice people?" Richard started to ask as many details as Rocky had. Finally Mal said, "Let's all sit down and discuss this properly."

"I will make the tea and biscuits," said Mue.

"And I will feed the dogs. I am sure they are hungry," said Mal. "Then we can all chat and find out what happened to everyone."

Mue brought in tea and chocolate biscuits for Richard, Mal, and herself. She brought some water and really nice dog biscuits for Jack and Rocky. (Because dogs are not allowed chocolate biscuits, and they don't like tea!) After they had all eaten Mal told Rocky that he could ask one question, and then Richard could then ask another. So this is how it went. Rocky asked about his mum and sisters. They were all doing well and now living in London. Richard asked where Rocky got to after he chased the cat. Rocky told him how he could not find his way home and lived with the foxes, who taught him the best way to survive in the forest. On and on they went until everybody had their questions answered and they were all happy.

Richard asked Rocky if he would like to come back with him to live in London.

"I don't think so because I like the open fields and the countryside. I love to chase rabbits and anything else that runs. I don't think I would like to live in a big town." Richard said that he was over here on business and was looking for a place to buy, so that he could stay here when he was in Ireland. He told Rocky, Mue and Mal that there was a place for sale just nearby and he was planning to buy it. "We will see you lots of times when we are over here. Next time I will bring Bea and the girls. Maybe," Richard continued, "you would all like to come to London for a holiday sometime and stay with us. We have a big house."

"Yes, Yes," said Rocky "that would be great fun to go for a holiday." Mal and Mue thought that it would be great too. "We always wanted to see London," said Mue.

"Great said Richard that's it settled. I hope to see you all soon. I will tell Bea you will all be coming

over to stay for a while." Richard said his goodbyes and got into his car. He waved out the window and hooted his horn as he drove off. "See you soon!" he shouted, "Bye, bye."

Richard had no sooner gone until there was another knock at the door; again Mue opened it. There was a small, fat man standing on the step. He had a chain around his neck, with some sort of a medal on it.

"I am the Lord Mayor of Whitehead," he announced. "I am here to give Rocky a medal for his bravery."

"OH, said Moo, I will call him now." But Rocky had followed her to the door and was standing right behind her. "Thank you very much," he said. "I really do not deserve it." Rocky was so pleased he put his medal on right away to show to all the other dogs.

Of course everyone made a great fuss of Rocky, except for one dog and its owner. They were jealous! This was an old mongrel called Jake and his owner, called Jacob. Jake was a cross old black and white mongrel who liked no one and no other dog. He lived just down the road a little, and would bark at anybody and anything that passed by his gate. Old Jacob would run out when he heard Jake barking and would shout at whoever passed. "Stay away from my gate you horrible lot." Old Jacob and old Jake decided to do something horrible to Rocky because everybody liked him, and that made them angry.

Jacob and Jake hatched a plan between them to make Rocky look bad. But first they had to lure him into their shed at the bottom of the garden beside the lettuce patch. Jacob grew all his own vegetables because he did not like going into shops and meeting other people. They waited until they saw Rocky walking down the road on his own. Jake said to Jacob "Right, let's get this plan into action!"

"Let's go now. I just can't wait to get at Rocky" replied Jacob. Jake walked out to meet Rocky. He said "Hi Rocky, could you help me please?"

"Of course," said Rocky, "What do you need help with? My master is trapped in the shed at the bottom of our garden and as I am not as strong as you are I can't pull the door open."

"Show me where it is," Rocky said. "I will open it

for you." Rocky followed Jake to the garden. When they reached the shed, Jake saw two Rabbits eating the lettuce nearby. I hate those Rabbits he said and gave chase. Of course he could not catch them; they were much too quick. Rocky just stood and watched, because he knew those two rabbits from the big field - one of which was the cheeky one Rocky was now friends with.

Rocky said, "Well they are away now, let's get your master out." Rocky went over to the shed door and got the handle between his teeth. He pulled and the door opened with ease. Rocky thought "That's strange! It was so easy to open a mouse could have done it." Inside was old Jacob.

"Thank you Rocky," he said, Come over to me and I will give you a biscuit for opening that door." When Rocky went into the shed for the biscuit old Jacob ran out closing the door quickly behind him. "Got you Rocky," he shouted,

"You're not so smart now."

"Let me out right now," barked Rocky. "We will, when we are ready," said Jake.

"Now let's get on with the rest of the plan" the two chuckled, as they walked back up the garden path.

Rocky looked all around the shed. It was dark inside and he could hardly see anything apart from one small window which was too high for even Rocky to jump up to. He could feel some garden tools, and an old sack. He thought he might as well get some sleep; maybe they would let him out in the morning.

Meanwhile Jacob had been making a coat for Jake. It was made of fur and was the same colour as Rocky's. He fitted it on to Jake who was about the same size as Rocky. It fitted well. Jacob strapped it on underneath.

"There you go Jake; everybody will think you are Rocky." The next morning Jake went along the road wearing the coat, and everybody was saying "Hi Rocky," and "Good morning Rocky." Jake stopped outside the butchers shop. Jacob was nearby but pretended he was not with him. Jake ran into the shop and jumped onto the counter. He grabbed a long line of sausages and ran up the road with them trailing behind him. The butcher was furious. "Stop that thief. That's Rocky, he stole my sausages," he shouted.

"Yes he did. I saw him too," said old Jacob, who was now standing outside the shop. "It was that

bad dog Rocky. Get the police." Jake was still running along the road. "All the people watched in amazement as he ran pass. They were saying, "There goes Rocky, he has turned into a bad dog. He has stolen all the sausages."

Jake ate some of the sausages and then left the rest in an entry. Then he met up with Jacob as planned. Jacob took off the "Rocky" coloured coat and stuffed it into his pocket. They both walked down the street together as if nothing had happened.

The next day they did the same thing, only this time it was the fish shop. Jake ran in dressed as Rocky again and took the biggest Salmon in the place. Everybody thought it was Rocky stealing again and called the police. The police stopped all the cars in the town! Nobody knew why they did that. It caused such a terrible traffic jam. It seems that is what the police do when they aren't sure what else to do. Everybody in the town hated Rocky! Everybody was saying what a bad dog he was. If he got caught they would lock him up in jail.

Meanwhile the real Rocky was getting very hungry because neither Jacob nor Jake had fed him. In fact they never even went to check he was alright in the shed.

Word was getting around about Rocky turning bad. Mal and Mue could not understand this behaviour. They had not seen him now for days. "Something must have happened to him," said Mue,

"Yes," said Mal "It's not like Rocky to do such things, and then not to come home. He knows how we worry about him because we love him so much."

"What can we do?" said Mue. "Everybody hates him now. Even the police are searching for him."

"I just don't know," said Mal, but knowing Rocky he will be OK wherever he is."

The rabbits heard about what was happening from the crows, which were told by the frogs that lived near the river. The cheeky rabbit said, "The last time I saw Rocky was with that old bad dog Jake and his master Jacob. They were at the shed near the lettuce patch. I wonder," he said to himself, and ran off shouting,

"Come on boys, we have a job to do."

All the rabbits followed, and when they reached the shed they took cover under the hedge - in case Jake was about. They could not see anyone around. The cheeky rabbit ran up to the shed door.

"Rocky, Rocky!" he called. Rocky heard the rabbit but was very weak from the lack of food. He tried to call back but couldn't even manage a bark. "Rocky, Rocky!" he heard the rabbit call again. Then he heard the rabbit say to his friends, "Well we tried. He must not be in there. Let's go home." Rocky thought, "I must do something or I will die in here." Rocky summoned up enough strength to knock over a rake which was leaning against the inside of the shed. It made a clattering noise as it crashed down to the floor.

"Did you hear that boys?" Said the rabbit. "Rocky's in there, let's get digging." All the rabbits starting burrowing at the back of the shed. Rabbits live underground and know how to dig fast with their sharp claws. Soon they were inside the shed and found Rocky who had had no food or water for almost a week now. They pulled him out through the hole, and down to the river, which was on the other side of the hedge. He drank some water. One of the rabbits had found the sausages

Jake had dropped in the entry. He brought them to Rocky, who ate the lot. Soon Rocky was on his feet again. He thanked all the rabbits for saving his life and setting him free. The rabbits told Rocky what the two rascals had been doing while he was in the shed. "Rocky," they said, "you will have to think of a plan to clear your name."

Rocky was thinking, "I have a plan and I will need your help again." He told the rabbits and they all laughed and said "Ok Rocky that will be fun, we will help." They all watched from behind the shed and saw Jacob and Jake arriving home. They were laughing and talking about all the things that they had done to Rocky. "He will not be able to show his face in town again," Jake said as they entered the house. Rocky waited a while until they were both sitting in the living room. He then showed himself at the window and barked loudly. "That's Rocky at the window," shouted Jacob. "It can't be," said Jake. "Let's go to the shed and check, he must have escaped." Rocky had run behind the shed again where the rabbits were hiding.

Jake and Jacob rushed down the garden path, only to find the shed was still locked. "He must be in there," they both said together. "Well there is only one way to be sure," said Jacob. Taking the keys from his pocket he opened the door. They both looked in but there was no sign of Rocky. "I'll bet he is hiding under that old rug over there." The two went into the shed towards the rug, and just as they were looking under it, the door slammed behind them. Rocky and the Rabbits had pushed the door shut. When Rocky stood on his hind legs he could reach the lock. He pushed the bar across with his nose.

"That's it," he barked. "We have them." Jake and Jacob were shouting and thumping at the wooden door.

"Let us out. It was only a joke. We just did it for a laugh Rocky. We were going to let you out soon." "Well," barked Rocky "let's see how you like it in there without any food or water. Just see if you find that so funny!" Rocky ran off barking "I will be back soon."

He walked into the police station, and told the policeman who he was and what had happened. The police man knew all about the incident and told Rocky he was under arrest for being a bad dog. Rocky told him he was innocent and did not do any of the things everybody accused him of. He told the policeman that he had been locked up in a shed all that time, and that old Jake had dressed up as Rocky to commit the crimes.

"So where are they now?" asked the policeman. "They are locked up in the shed. Come and see for yourself." Rocky and all the policemen got into their cars and roared off down the road. When they came to Jake's place, they all went to the shed. "Are you in there Jacob?" asked the policeman. "Yes," came a voice that bad dog Rocky locked us in just as we were getting some firewood." The police man glared at Rocky,

"This had better not be true." They opened the shed door and out stepped Jacob and Jake. "You bad dog Rocky. Why did you lock us in the shed?" Rocky then said to the policeman, "Have a look in his pocket." The police man told Jacob to turn out his pockets, and can you guess what he found? Yes, he found the coat made to look like Rocky's that fitted Jake.

"You two are under arrest. You will both go to jail for doing all these bad things to Rocky. You are free to go Rocky, and I will tell all the people in the town you are innocent of these crimes. Everybody

will trust you again." said the policeman.

That evening there was a knock on the door. "Can I speak to Rocky?" a voice asked. Rocky came out. It was the butcher, he had brought with him the biggest bone he could find, and a kilo of sausages all for Rocky.

He said how sorry he was that he had accused Rocky in the wrong and hoped that this would make up for it. Next the fishmonger arrived with the biggest Salmon ever to be seen in Whitehead. "This is for Rocky," he said, "Tell him I am very sorry." Rocky was not too keen on fish so he gave the Salmon to Mal and Mue. That night they sat around the table and had a great feed each. They all laughed at how bad old Jacob and Jake had been caught.

Later that night just before bedtime Mal announced that they were all going to the Caravan in the morning for a few days to relax. Rocky went to sleep that night dreaming of the beautiful beach to run on and the forest to explore at Castlerock.

ROCKY GOES TO CASTLEROCK

The next morning everyone was up bright and early. The sun was shining and Rocky could hear the sausages sizzling in the pan for breakfast. He had a good long sleep and was ready for the journey to the Caravan at Castlerock. After they all had breakfast, the car was filled with the many bits and pieces that were needed. Rocky made sure he brought his bone with him, because there were still lots of chewing to be done on it.

They set off at ten o'clock and arrived at Castlerock Holiday Park about eleven thirty. Rocky loved it there, he would watch the children playing on the swings and slides, they were all so happy. It was really well kept and a very nice place to be for a holiday. He knew all the people who worked there. Leanne and Sandra who worked in the office. Hugh and David who kept the grass cut, and of course Steven the boss.

They all patted and made a fuss of Rocky when they saw him. The journey itself had been uneventful, only a few dogs to look at and a cat or two passing. Rocky wished he could jump out of the window when he saw the cats. He really wanted to chase them. But then he remembered what happened the last time he ran after a cat.

At Castlerock Mal put away all the goods they had brought, and Mue took Rocky to the forest. Rocky was having a great time playing in and out of the hedges, looking for something to chase. Suddenly he heard this very deep loud bark. Rocky came out of the hedge to see what had made that sound. It was a huge dog just in front of Mue. His master was walking beside him. The dog was so large Rocky only reached up to his chest.

"My goodness I have never seen a dog so big," thought Rocky. "I wonder if he is friendly." Rocky slowly walked up the giant dog.

"Hi there," he barked. The dog looked down at Rocky,

"Hi little fellow," said the huge dog. "How did you get to be so big?" Rocky asked.

"It's just the way I am. We are all big dogs, but sadly there are not many of us left. We grew too big and nobody wanted us. We are too expensive to feed and look after. Even other dogs won't play with us because they think we would hurt them. I

am very sad and lonely," said the dog. "Will you play with me?"

"Of course I will," said Rocky. "I am not afraid of anything. What's your name?"

"Everybody calls me Irish, because I am an Irish Wolf Hound. I think I am the biggest dog in the world."

"Wow said Rocky; imagine me meeting the biggest dog in the world. Can I have your autograph?" (That was like we humans asking for a famous person's autograph.) The big dog pressed his paw into the ground which left a good print.

Rocky was pleased. He then asked "Are you a wolf?"

"No, no," said Irish. "Many years ago when there were lots of wolves in Ireland the farmers kept us to chase them away from the herds of cattle and sheep, because the wolves would kill and eat them. But we did such a good job that there are no wolves left in Ireland now - or at least so few that we are no longer needed." Rocky barked "OK, let's play for a while." Rocky ran down the forest path, shouting, "Well come on then, try and catch me."

Irish barked "That's easy, my legs are four times longer than yours I could catch you in no time."

"Well then, let's see you do it!" Rocky barked back. Meanwhile Mue was chatting to the owner of Irish. They were talking about their dogs, and the owner said, "I have never seen Irish have so much fun. Most dogs run away when they see her." They watched the two dogs running along the path. Rocky would make a quick turn into the trees or bushes every time Irish got close. No matter how much Irish tried she could not catch Rocky.

"Oh you are much too fast and slippery for me," she said, sitting down panting. Rocky thought to himself that those Wolves must not have been very smart to let that big dog catch them. Rocky sat down beside her. "Well I thought you said it would be easy to catch me."

"I was wrong, said Irish, "I don't think I could ever catch you. Will you play with me again sometime Rocky? I really enjoyed the chase."

"Anytime we meet in the forest we'll have fun." Rocky answered. The man and his dog went on their way and Mue and Rocky went on theirs.

A bit further on Rocky spotted a rabbit, then a

hare. The hare was very fast, but Rocky still gave chase. It was soon into it's lair and back to safety. Rocky then saw a squirrel and of course he ran after it, but the squirrel ran up a tree and disappeared among the branches and leaves. Mue said "It's time to go back to the Caravan now." Rocky had great fun in the forest that day, and was looking forward to going back again; maybe meet Irish again or make another new friend.

The next morning was not so bright. There had been lots of rain through the night, and it was still very cloudy. Rocky looked out the window, "Might as well go back to bed he thought. Nothing to do on a day like that." Mal and Mue had breakfast. Rocky got up quickly when he smelt the sausages cooking. (Rocky just loved his sausages.)

"What will we do today Mue?" Rocky heard Mal asking. "What about going back to Benvarden, the dog home, and showing Louise how Rocky is getting on with us?" Mue suggested.

"Great idea," said Mal, we will leave at ten o'clock."

They set off just after ten and arrived at Benvarden before eleven. Louise was in the yard washing down an Alsatian which had rolled himself in all kinds of muck. They heard her saying to the dog, "Now you behave yourself in future because you will never get a home smelling like that." Rocky gave a bark; Louise looked up, and recognized Rocky straight away.

"Hi Rocky, Hi Mal, Hi Mue," she shouted. "How are you all doing? Is this fellow behaving himself?" They all started chatting among themselves. Rocky decided to have a look around to see if any of his old friends were still there. No, there was no one he knew, "That's good," he thought, "they must have all got homes."

Rocky was about to leave the dog area, when he heard a whimper, like a dog crying. He turned to investigate. Rocky looked into one of the sheds where he could see a little dog all curled up in one of the corners and it was crying.

"What's wrong?" asked Rocky, "Don't cry you will soon get a home too." The little dog without even turning or opening it's eyes told Rocky that she had a home but the people were bad to her, and beat her. She said that she had run away but got caught again and that's why she was back here. She told Rocky that she did not want a home

again, because she did not trust any humans except Louise. Rocky thought the voice was a bit familiar.

"Are you a Beagle dog?"

"Yes I am," she said.

"Do you not remember me? I was here too. It's Rocky." She turned around.

"Rocky," she said, "I thought I would never see you again. I love you so much."

"I have looked everywhere for you Betsy, so at last we meet again, and this time we will not be parted. I will speak to Mal and Mue and get them to look after you."

"OH Rocky, Rocky, Rocky I am so happy."

BETSY COMES TO CASTLEROCK

Rocky ran out of the dog area and found Mal and Mue still chatting to Louise. Rocky wondered how he could let them know. He decided to run around them in circles to get their attention. Mue and Mal looked at Rocky. Mue said "What is it Rocky? Do you want something?" Rocky turned and walked away a little, as if to get her to follow. Mue was not too sure what he wanted, but started to follow anyway. Rocky led the way into the shed, and Mue saw Betsy in the corner.

"Ah you poor little dog," she said. "You are all alone, and you have been crying." Rocky went beside Betsy and started to rub himself against her.

"OH I see now," said Mue." "You want a partner to play with. Well I shall speak to Mal and we will see if we can bring her home." Mal agreed it would be nice if Rocky had a friend of his own. He reckoned they could hunt and play together. Mue signed all the paperwork at the office and Betsy jumped into the car beside Rocky. Rocky was telling her all about the Caravan Park and Castlerock the whole

way back. Betsy was a well mannered dog, she kept herself in good condition, combed her hair every day, and never spoke out of turn. Rocky decided she must be a pedigree beagle just like his mum.

The next day, after breakfast Rocky asked Mue if he could show Betsy the beach and maybe play for a while. "I will be good," he barked, "I promise I will not let Betsy out of my sight and I won't get into any trouble."

"Well OK then, if you promise," said Mue. "Mal and I are going to Crusoe's for coffee."

They both loved the coffee at Crusoe's because it was the best for miles around. And the food was always fresh and tasty. But be back here for lunch at twelve." Mue added. Rocky and Betsy ran off. They had to cross the railway line before getting to the beach, and Rocky noticed that there was a train waiting at the platform with its doors open. Rocky said to Betsy "Let's see what it's like inside the train. I love to chase trains but I have never seen inside one."

"Well if you think its safe Rocky?" said Betsy.

"Of course it's safe; I am only having a quick look.

What harm can that do?" Rocky and Betsy sneaked passed the ticket collector and up to the train. This was the closest they had ever been to the huge engine. It was one of the old type engines which were driven by steam. It was usually kept in an engine shed at Whitehead, but once a year they let it have a good run out, and this time it had come to Castlerock. Rocky said to Betsy, "Come on, let's get inside. It looks like fun."

"OH Rocky you promised you would not get into any trouble."

"Come on, we will only be a few minutes." Betsy jumped into the carriage. It was old inside but very well made. Lots of polished wood and large soft seats. Rocky was sitting in one of the very best seats looking out the window. Suddenly the big engine gave a whistle and a loud puffing noise and then the carriage shuddered and started to move forward.

"OH," Rocky barked, "Betsy we are in trouble now alright. We don't even know where this train will take us." Rocky looked out of the window again.

"The train is going too fast for us to jump out," he said, "So we will have to stay on until the end of

the journey -wherever that might be." They heard the ticket collector coming down the corridor.

"Quick!" he barked. "Get under the seat." The two dogs hid as the ticket collector passed by shouting "Tickets please. Everyone must have a ticket." They stayed under the seat for a while and with the rocking of the train they both felt very sleepy. Soon they were fast asleep.

Rocky felt the train coming to a halt. "Wake up, Betsy! Wake up," he said, "we are stopping somewhere." Betsy woke with a start.

"Oh," she said "I was having a lovely dream about you and me getting married and having lots of pups." Rocky looked at her, and thought to himself that no way was marriage for him.

"Well sorry," he said, "for having to waken you but we had better get off this train."

"Where are we now?" asked Betsy. "Look at the time. It's after one o'clock; we are in big trouble with Mue, because she told us to be home by twelve for lunch."

"Well come on then, we had better get off quickly before this train goes any further." Lots of people

were getting off at this station, so Rocky and Betsy hid between them so that the ticket collector would not see them. They saw a big sign at the station. It read PORTRUSH. "Well this is where we are now," said Rocky.

"Great," said Betsy. "Now how do we get home?"

"I really don't know," said Rocky. "I have never been to Portrush before and I don't know how long we were asleep. We could be miles away from Castlerock and the Caravan. But don't worry Betsy I will find the way. Come with me into the town. Follow all the other people." They followed the crowds of people until they came to a place called, Barry's Amusement Park. Rocky saw a train there and thought, "Right this must be the train back again. Jump on," he told Betsy.

"That's a funny looking train," said Betsy. It's all colours and has a little bell on each carriage. And look, there are only little boys and girls on it. Do you think we should get on Rocky?"

"Of course," said Rocky, "Let's try it." They both got on the funny little train, and with a whistle, off it went. It went round in a circle, then under a tunnel and round again in a circle and after ten

minutes it stopped again at the same place they had boarded.

"Well," said Betsy. "That was no good for us."

"No," said Rocky. "But it was fun, let's try those cars over there; maybe they are going to Castlerock. They saw a sign above the cars saying DODGEMS, "Look," said Rocky "that word looks like Dog-ems."

"Must be for us then," said Betsy. They jumped on to the seat of one, just as it started to go. The little car was going all over the place, to the right, then to the left, then round in circles.

"Grab the steering wheel Rocky," shouted Betsy. Bang, Bang, Bang, two other cars had bumped into them.

"I'll get those boys," said Rocky, and aimed his Dodgem straight at their car. BANG! He hit one, making it spin round in circles. Another one hit Rocky from behind. Rocky spun around and rammed into the other boy's car. Everybody was laughing and having great fun. BANG, BANG. On they went until the time was up and the cars stopped.

"That was super fun," said Rocky.

"Glad YOU think so," snapped Betsy, who was still shaking from the experience. Rocky looked behind him, he could see one of the attendants running towards him shouting.

"Hey you, where's your ticket to get in here?"

"Run, run, run fast!" barked Rocky to Betsy, "I think we have been caught. Follow me." Rocky ran for the nearest door. Betsy followed and they both got a terrible shock when they looked into the mirror which was just inside the door. Rocky was six times taller than he really was, and Betsy was very small and fat.

"What has happened to us? Why do we look like this?" said Betsy in a panic. "I don't know," said Rocky, "Look into that other mirror over there; you are very long and thin. Look at me I am now small and fat in that mirror. I think it's a hall of different mirrors making you look tall, fat or thin. It's great fun. Let's look into them all." Rocky and Betsy laughed and laughed as they walked around seeing themselves in all funny shapes. Rocky looked into a plain mirror and suddenly froze. There behind him was the park attendant, just

ready to grab him. Rocky quickly pulled himself together and barked, "Betsy he's here again. Run." Again Rocky and Betsy ran out of one door and in through another.

They found themselves running up lots of steps. Round and round they went until they got to the top. At the top there was nowhere to go except down a big slide.

"OK," said Rocky, "he will never catch us now." They both jumped onto the slide. "Where will this take us?" asked Betsy.

"I don't know," said Rocky but isn't this terrific!" Round and round they went, faster and faster down the slide.

"Wheeeeee," barked Rocky "This is fantastic." But suddenly he saw the attendant at the bottom of the slide with a big sack.

"OH! NO!" shouted Rocky, trying to stop, but he was going too fast. The attendant held out the sack and Rocky fell into it with a bump, then Betsy bumped in beside him.

"Got you now, you naughty dogs." The attendant closed the bag and walked all the way back to the

train station. He told the driver of the train to take these naughty dogs back to Castlerock and to tell the police what they had been up to. Later that night the police came to the Caravan. "I have two very naughty dogs in this bag, the policeman said sternly. "I believe they belong to you and Mal." He opened the bag and there was Rocky and Betsy looking very sorry for themselves.

"Yes they are our dogs," said Mue. "We have been looking everywhere for them."

"Well," said the policeman, "You had better have a word with them, because if I catch them again, they will be put into a dog home."

"I will!" said Mue.

After the policeman left the two naughty dogs were sent straight to bed with no supper.

"Ah well," said Rocky to Betsy, "It was worth it for all the fun we had."

"I'm starving," said Betsy. "And it's all your fault, wanting to look inside trains indeed."

"Ah," said Rocky, "Don't worry. I have a couple of bones and a few pigs' ears hidden under my rug just in case I had a situation like this."

"OH Rocky, you are the greatest. You think of everything". The two ate their bones and pigs ears and then settled down for the night. Rocky whispered "I wonder where the other train goes? The one that goes the other way."

"Don't you dare even think of it. We are in enough trouble as it is." Soon they were fast asleep and Rocky was dreaming of all the fun he had that day. Betsy was just glad to be home again and in her warm cozy bed.

ROCKY AND BETSY GO TO A DOG SHOW

The next morning Rocky and Betsy came for breakfast. "Right you two, what happened to you both yesterday? You know we were very worried about you."

"Oh," said Rocky, "it was my entire fault. I just wanted to see inside a train and then it started to go, and we could not get off as it was going too quickly." Rocky went on to tell them of all that had happened. "We meant to come straight home again but got lost in this fun fair called Barrie's. It was awful on those Dog-ems (as Rocky called them) and the other rides we had to go on to try and find our way home." All the time Betsy knew he was telling lies because he had loved all the fun.

"Well," said Mue, "You are both forgiven this time. Please do not do that again without letting us know where you are going. Now eat your sausages because we are taking you both to a big dog show. All the best dogs in the country will be there. So Rocky you behave - if you can. I know I

can trust you Betsy but that Rocky one is always up to some mischief."

Betsy turned to Rocky and said, "Wow a dog show! I must look my very best."

Rocky replied, "Huh! don't be so silly just a lot of pansy dogs prancing about."

"Have you ever been to a dog show Rocky?" asked Betsy.

"No I haven't, and I don't want to go to one either."

"Well you had better be on your best behaviour because Mal and Mue will be very angry with you if you disgrace them at this show. Especially as you were so bad yesterday."

"Yea, Yea." said Rocky, "I get the picture. I'll behave."

About one o'clock they all arrived at the show. Betsy looked really lovely; she had washed, combed her hair and tied a pink bow around her neck. Rocky was just his usual scruffy self. They walked around with Mal and Mue looking at all the different stalls. One was selling dog shampoo; Betsy said "Doesn't it smell gorgeous?"

"Huh," said Rocky "I think they should drop the sham bit and just call it poo because that's what's I think it smells like."

"Oh Rocky, cheer up a bit, try to enjoy the show." Rocky was not in a good mood. Then they heard the loud speaker announcing, "The most glamorous dog competition is about to start. Would any dog wanting to compete please come to gate seven now?"

"Oh can I enter please?" asked Betsy. "Yes of course you can," said Mue. "We will all go with you." They stopped at gate seven where an official was taking down the names of all the dogs. "And what is your name?" he asked Betsy.

"It's Betsy," she said a little shyly. "Take a seat over there, said the official, and the judge will be along shortly." Betsy looked around her. There were all sorts of dogs. Some with bows in their hair, others with small white boots on. Even Betsy thought they looked silly. Imagine dogs with boots on! Betsy was a bit nervous.

"Don't worry," said Rocky, "You will knock them all dead." That was Rocky's way of saying "You are the best looking dog of them all." The judge

came into the hall. There were about one hundred dogs and crowds of people who had come to watch. Rocky was bored and wandered off when nobody was looking. They were all too interested in the competition to notice. Rocky heard another announcement over the loud speaker. It was saying. "Any dog for the Rough and Tumble Twenty Mile race please come to gate twenty four."

"Now that sounds like fun," thought Rocky, and headed for the gate.

He was asked his name when he arrived by the race official.

"Rocky," he told the man.

"Right Rocky, line up with the others, we will be starting soon." Rocky took a place at the starting line. He looked at his competitors. Some were quite small. Others were strong looking dogs, but a bit fat. However there was one, which was a greyhound and he looked thin and mean. The big greyhound was looking all around him too and laughing at his opponents.

"I win this race every year," he barked at all the other dogs. "You have no chance of beating me

because I'm the fastest dog alive." Rocky took a really long look at him this time. He was called a greyhound, but he was black all over. Rocky barked back at him,

"Hey you, you should have been called a black hound instead of a greyhound. You look silly." The big hound was getting cross at Rocky's insults. "I will show you who is the silly one at the end of this race when I win."

The official came over to the lineup, and addressed the twenty five dogs there.

"This is a twenty mile race from Castlerock to Limavady. It's all cross country, through forests, fields, and rivers. There are no rules about how you get there except that you cannot use trains, buses, or cars or any other means of transport. It's a very tough race for the toughest and fastest dogs only! There is no set route, so the first dog to run up Main Street in Limavady to the town hall wins. The winner will receive a special prize later at the prize giving ceremony. It will be held at the dog show around six pm tonight. Ready," the official shouted. "Get on your marks." He held up a starting pistol and fired it into the air. The noise made Rocky jump. All the dogs set off as fast as

they could. The big black greyhound was already in the lead. Rocky was last to get started as the noise from the starting pistol had shocked him. He had not been expecting that to happen. Rocky ran for all he was worth, and was beginning to catch up on the pack of dogs ahead. He passed one, then two. Next he caught up on another one and passed it as well.

Rocky could not see the greyhound now as he was so far in front. He kept running, he passed more dogs 4/5/6/7 dogs. Faster and faster he ran and passed 8/9/10/11/12 dogs. Now he was catching up. Rocky noticed some dogs that were walking back to the show. They were exhausted, and had given up. Then, there right in front of him he saw the big greyhound running, but not at full speed. Rocky began to catch up with him. He was now almost at his heels. The big grey looked round and couldn't believe his eyes when he saw Rocky so close. Rocky put on an extra burst of energy. He started to overtake the big grey. The grey then did the same and passed Rocky. Rocky pushed himself harder and harder.

It was not that Rocky wanted the prize which kept him going, but the thought of beating that greyhound and making him look silly. Rocky started to come along side again. The big grey was flat out now going as fast as he could "I am going to lose this race," thought the grey, "And I can't let that happen. I will have to do something. This dog is faster than I am." The big grey put on one last burst of energy. He was nearly exhausted. He passed Rocky but knew that he could not keep up this pace. Rocky was still going strong. It was now neck and neck. The big grey pushed a little further in front, and then with his back paws kicked up some dirt into Rocky's eyes. Rocky was blinded by the dirt.

"You cheat!" Rocky shouted. "You rotten cheat!"

The big grey just laughed as Rocky was forced to stop.

"I will win," barked the grey "You do look silly Rocky." Soon the big Grey was out of sight.

Rocky sat at the side of the forest path. He was rubbing his eyes, but he still could see nothing. He heard other dogs passing, barking- "Look at Rocky, he has given up or else he must be exhausted."

Rocky could do nothing. He had to wait there until

his eyes cleared, and goodness knows how long that would take. Suddenly he heard a sound in the forest behind him. A voice called "Hi Rocky. I saw what the grey did to you. You could have out run him easily."

"Yes," said Rocky, "I would have if he had not cheated."

"Well, two can play at that game." said the voice.

"I know that voice," said Rocky. "Who are you?"

"Do you not remember me? I am Irish, the wolfhound."

"Yes," said Rocky. "You are my friend. But how can I win now? He must be miles in front of me."

"Well, there is about another ten miles to go and its rough country. There is also a wide river to cross, which might slow him up a bit. Now let's stop talking and get passed him." said Irish. "You get on my back and hold on tight." Rocky jumped on, and gripped his paws around the Wolfhound's neck.

"Right let's go." Irish started to run, slowly at first, then faster and faster. Rocky could feel the wind on his face. It was getting stronger and stronger the faster Irish went. Irish knew the forest well,

and knew the best place to cross the river. He jumped over dead trees lying on the ground. He jumped over ditches which any other dog would have had to go around. They came to the river.

"Hold tight Rocky. We are going to swim now."

"Oh great," said Rocky." I love swimming, but I wish I could see where I was going first." The big Wolfhound jumped into the water and started to swim. The water was splashing into Rocky's eyes and clearing out the dirt. By the time they got to the other side Rocky's eyes had cleared well and he could see better again.

"Just a little further," said Irish. "Then I will let you down, and you can run up Main Street to the town hall, as if nothing had happened. I will hide so nobody will see me." They came to a hole in the hedge.

"OK Rocky. This is where you get off. Just keep running straight ahead. That is Main Street." Rocky thanked Irish and jumped down. He looked through the hole first, to see if anybody was about. In the distance, in front of him, was the Grey. He was heading for the main street, but looked very tired. Rocky had had a good rest on Irish's back,

and was feeling wonderful. He ran up behind him, and then overtook him at full speed. The grey could not believe what he was seeing.

"What was that?" Rocky passed the grey so quickly he did not even get a good look at him. Then he saw it was Rocky.

"OH no! Not him again! It couldn't be. He was miles behind me." The big Grey was too tired to run any further and just had to lie down. Rocky passed the post at the town hall, and all the people cheered.

"Rocky is the fastest dog alive," they shouted.

"Rocky wins the toughest ever dog's race." Most of the other dogs had given up, except a little Poodle, who should not have been in the race, but she just took it easily from the start, thinking, "All these other dogs will get tired, and have to give up, and I will win." She passed the post next, after Rocky, and was given second place.

"Now who looks silly!" laughed Rocky. "Imagine being beaten by a Poodle! You silly big Black hound." Rocky kept on teasing the Grey. The Grey was too tired even to answer Rocky and just fell asleep where he was lying. Rocky was driven back

to the show by one of the officials. He found Mal and Mue, who told him how well Betsy had done in the beauty competition. "Where did you get to Rocky? We were looking for you everywhere.

"Oh I was just running around," he said. "Well come on then. Let's see where all the prizes are being given out." They all walked over to a tent which had a big notice outside which read, "Collect your prize here." Inside a man was calling out all the names of the prize winners. Just as they came in and got a seat, the man called out, "Betsy the Beagle." Betsy was a bit shy, but she managed to walk slowly towards the front of the tent where the man was standing.

"Betsy you have won the cup for the most beautiful dog." He handed down the cup, and inside it was a big succulent bone with lots of meat on it.

"OH! Thank you so much," said Betsy and she carried the cup and bone back to her place. She felt so proud, and hoped all the other dogs were jealous. Mal and Mue were delighted and hugged and patted her, telling her what a good dog she was.

"Not like you Rocky. Always getting into some

kind of trouble." Rocky just sat still and said nothing. The official called out a few more dogs' names for prizes. Then he said, "Well, that's all folks. There are no more prizes to be given out." Rocky was very upset.

"I won that race," he said to himself, "And I should be getting a prize." Just as everyone was about to leave another official came into the tent. "Wait everybody," he announced. "We have one more prize, and it's the biggest and best prize of all! It's for the dog who won the toughest race. Twenty miles from Castlerock to Limavady. The greatest and the fastest dog in Castlerock and maybe in the whole world is ROCKY!" he shouted at the top of his voice.

"ROCKY, come here to get your prize."

Everyone gasped in amazement, including Mal, Mue, and Betsy.

"You never told us you had entered the competition," said all three of them together. Rocky said nothing and sauntered up to the front to collect his prize. The cup was so big that it took Mal and Mue to carry it between them. Of course Rocky got a big meaty bone too. Rocky thanked

the man, and under his breath, so as nobody could hear, he said thanks to Irish for helping him win. When people asked Rocky what he thought about winning such a huge cup, he would say, "Never mind the cup, the bone was much better!"

Later on they all went home, and everybody was happy with their day out at the dog show.

BETSY COMES TO WHITEHEAD

A few more days passed by in Castlerock. Rocky and Betsy were on their best behaviour. They played in the sand digging holes and hiding anything they could find. Sometimes Rocky would go for a swim.

He would shout to Betsy, "Come on in, its lovely in here, just like a warm bath." Betsy knew he was telling her fibs, as she had gone in for a paddle and the water was really cold. Betsy was happy where she was, playing on the sand. She did not like the water too much anyway. She always got a bit frightened when the waves came over her head. Betsy would run to the shore and give herself a good shake. But Rocky was tough and loved the water - even if it was cold.

Mal and Mue announced that they would all have to go to Whitehead soon, as there were things they had to attend to. Betsy said, "Whitehead, where is that Rocky?"

Rocky answered saying, "You will find out soon. It's also a great place to have fun. There are lots of rocks, and pools in the rocks to catch crabs for tea."

"Yuck!" said Betsy, "I hope you don't expect me to eat crabs."

"You don't know what you're missing," chuckled Rocky. "Don't worry it's great and you will love it. I will show you all around the place, right up to the lighthouse."

"The lighthouse?" said Betsy quizzically. "What's a lighthouse?"

"Oh it's to help ships find their way in the dark," said Rocky, very proud of himself for knowing all this. At two pm that day they all piled into the car and headed for Whitehead. Of course Rocky and Betsy both fell fast asleep on the back seat. They woke as Mal and Mue were taking all the goods out of the car and into the apartment.

"This is nice," said Betsy, as she climbed the steps to the house. "Look at that lovely view all over Whitehead," she went on.

Rocky thought, "Yes. It is great for me to watch where all the cats hide." They slept well that night, and after breakfast, Rocky asked if he could show

Betsy around Whitehead.

"Well OK Rocky. But don't you get into any trains or get into any trouble."

"I won't," said Rocky, "I will behave."

"Promise me now Rocky. No chasing sheep or fighting with other dogs."

"I promise I won't do anything like that."

Off they both went, and Rocky said to Betsy, "Be very careful on the road, and don't go anywhere without me." Soon they were at the rocks. Rocky showed Betsy how to catch a crab, and how to break it's tough shell, to get at the tender meat underneath. Betsy did try a little after a lot of coaxing from Rocky. "Not so bad Rocky. You were right. I do like crab after all."

"Yes," said Rocky. "You have to try something before you say you don't like it. That's just silly."

Betsy looked up and asked, "Is that the lighthouse on the top of that hill?"

"It is," said Rocky. "Let's go that way now." They climbed lots of steps.

"There are about one hundred steps," Rocky told

Betsy. About half way up they came across a long rope hanging from a tree.

"Look," shouted Rocky, "some boys must have been using this as a swing."

"Let's have a go," barked Betsy. Rocky got the rope in his teeth first, and with his back legs pushed himself off the cliff. "This is great! Super," he barked and barked. Then Betsy had a go. Betsy was a lot more careful than Rocky. She didn't swing out so far. They spent about an hour swinging. Then Rocky said, "I'm hungry. Let's go home." They ran on a bit closer to the top of the cliff.

Suddenly Rocky stopped. "I smell food" he said. Rocky put his nose to the ground and started to sniff. He followed the scent of ham and cheese to a picnic basket on the ground. Rocky and Betsy looked all around, but there was no one about.

"I wonder who could have left that here?" said Betsy.

"I don't know," said Rocky. "I am wondering if they would miss a few sandwiches."

"ROCKY!" Betsy shouted. "That would be stealing."

"I know. But I am so hungry, and they have just left them lying here." Rocky lifted a ham sandwich and started to eat it. "OH I am so hungry." He was just about to start into another one when he heard someone shouting, "Help! Help!" Rocky looked at Betsy. "Did you hear that?"

"I did," said Betsy. "It sounded as if it was coming from over there." The two dogs looked over the cliff, and there half way up, were two people. A man and a woman who were trying to climb the cliff face and had got stuck. Rocky thought how stupid they were, as they had no safety equipment, no ropes or any essentials. They must have walked down the path, and decided to try to climb back up. He shouted to Betsy, "Come on. Let's get that rope we found earlier!" The two ran back down the path, until they came to where the rope was hanging from the tree branch. "I will have to climb up to the rope, and chew through the part that is tied to the tree," said Rocky.

Rocky climbed, holding tight with his claws until he reached the rope. Rocky chewed at the knot. His sharp teeth took no time to bite through the rope. It fell to the ground. Rocky came down the tree and told Betsy to grab one end between her teeth.

He did the same, and between them they managed to pull the long rope up the hill. At the top Rocky barked to Betsy, "Let's run round the big tree over there, at the edge of the cliff, and when we get the rope the same length at both ends we will drop it over to the climbers." The plan worked. They put it round the tree and dropped the two ends down the cliff. It was just long enough to reach the two climbers, who grabbed an end each.

"Now," shouted Rocky. "You both hold on until we find help."

"Come on Betsy, let's get home and tell Mal and Mue." On the way they were passing a field, when Rocky saw a tractor sitting with its engine running. "That's what we need. Let's borrow it." "Don't be silly Rocky. Neither you nor I can drive a tractor."

"It's probably just like one of those Dog-ems we drove."

"First thing, it's a DODGEM, not a Dog-em, and it will be a lot more difficult to drive than you think."

"Well let's try," barked Rocky, as he ran towards it.

Rocky jumped up onto the tractor. It was a lot

more complicated than he thought. There were levers everywhere. Rocky pulled one lever towards him. There was a loud noise and a big pulley thing started to move on the back of the tractor.

"Oops," Rocky said. "Not the right one." He then heard a boy shouting,

"Hey, you get off my tractor." The farmer's son who was about twelve years old came running up the field towards Rocky. "Get off that tractor at once. If my dad comes you will be in big trouble."

Then, as the boy got closer, he stopped and said, "Is that you Rocky?"

Rocky barked, "Yes it is me."

"You're that dog who saved the kids from drowning. Your picture was in the paper. That's how I know you. It's great to meet such a famous dog." Rocky barked and barked, and then he jumped down from the tractor. Rocky stood in front of it and tried to make the boy understand that he needed him to follow. The boy watched him for a while, and then said, "Do you need me to help you to do something Rocky?"

Rocky barked, and nodded his head. The boy got

into the cab of the tractor and followed Rocky and Betsy to the cliff edge.

There they stopped and looked over. The man and woman were still hanging onto the rope. The boy looked down and gasped. "I see now Rocky. You needed the tractor to pull these people up from the cliff." The boy tied the rope to the tractor and started to move forward very slowly. Soon the two people were at the top, and were very thankful to the boy for pulling them up.

"How did you know we were down there?" asked the man. The boy looked round.

"It was the two dogs who told me to come. They threw the rope down to you. They are the ones who saved your life." The man and woman looked all around, and the boy looked in the bushes, but nowhere could the two dogs been seen. Rocky and Betsy had run off home before the man and woman realized Rocky had stolen their sandwiches. They both got home in good time for dinner, and Mue was very pleased to see them.

"I hope you two did not get into any trouble today."

"Not a bit," said Rocky.

"I see on the news tonight that two dogs saved a couple of people at the cliff face."

"Is that right?" said Rocky.

"Anything to do with you pair?"

"Not us," replied Rocky and slipped off to bed without saying another word.

ROCKY MEETS MR HAWKINS

Rocky awoke to see the sun shining. It was going to be a very hot day. He barked over to Betsy who was still sleeping, "Come on sleepy head. Let's get up and go out to play. It's a lovely morning."

Betsy groaned, "What time is it?"

"It's just after seven." said Rocky.

"Go back to sleep. It's the middle of the night," Betsy barked back. Rocky tried to sleep a little more, but just couldn't manage, so he got out of his rug and went outside just to see what a beautiful a morning it was. The birds were singing and the flowers were in full bloom. Rocky thought "It's great to be alive. I wonder what I will do today? Maybe a bit of fishing." Rocky would sometimes go to the rock pools to see if any small fish had been abandoned there by the sea when the tide went out.

Rocky wondered about what he had just said - "When the tide went out." "But," he thought, "Where does it go to? Maybe to the other side of the world. Someday," he went on thinking, "I would like to go to the other side of the world, where everything must be upside down." Rocky laughed to himself at the thought of it. Imagine walking on your head with your feet in the air. He tried to stand on his front two paws to see what it would be like on the other side of the world.

"What are you doing?" asked a voice from inside the hedge.

"Oh, is that you cheeky rabbit?"

"Yes," said the rabbit. "What are you doing?" he asked again.

"I am learning to walk upside down because some day I want to go to the other side of the world."

"Oh I see," said the rabbit. "Well you look silly walking upside down on this side of the world." Before Rocky could answer him he heard Mue calling.

"Sausages are ready. Come on Rocky. Breakfast time, It's nine o'clock."

Rocky barked "Goodbye," to the rabbit and ran into the house. That was one thing Rocky did not want to miss. Betsy was already up and had started her breakfast.

"Hi Rocky, Where did you go?"

"Oh, I just took a walk, as it is such a lovely morning. Not like some dogs that lie in their beds!" Rocky teased Betsy.

"Well I was tired after all that excitement yesterday. I am going to do nothing today. I will sunbathe all day."

After breakfast Betsy lay down in the garden, and Rocky went fishing. He found two long eels in one of the pools. "Great," he said. "You're my dinner."

Rocky scooped up the eels with his paw, and then carried them home in his mouth. He set one beside Betsy.

"Your dinner," he announced.

"You must be joking," said Betsy. "That is disgusting. I hope you don't expect me to eat that slimy looking over-grown worm."

"Now, now," said Rocky. "What did I tell you about saying you don't like something before you have even tasted it?"

"Yes I know," barked Betsy, "but at this I draw the line. No way am I even going to try that. By the

way, what time is it?"

"It's nearly two o'clock now," said Rocky.

"Where can you get something cool, like ice cream or lollypops around here?" Betsy asked.

"I am not too sure, but I will ask in the town." Rocky ran down the road into Whitehead town. He saw one of his friends standing by a lamp post.

"Hi Lassie," Rocky barked.

"Where does one get some ice cream around here?" Lassie barked back, "You can get some at the shop which is about two miles down that road, or you can wait until Mr Hawkins arrives in the ice cream van. You see all those boys and girls standing there at the corner? Well, that's where the ice cream van stops every day, usually around this time." Rocky ran to the corner and waited. The boys and girls were very hot, and all were waiting on the ice cream coming to cool them down.

"He's late today," Rocky heard one boy saying. "I hope he hasn't broken down. It's far too hot. I think I am going to faint if I don't get my ice cream soon." said another little girl. Rocky thought to himself that maybe the van had broken down. "I

will run along the road to the shop and see if I can find him." Rocky ran along the road Lassie had pointed out to him.

About one mile away he came across the ice cream van. It was stuck in the hedge!

"What has happened?" Rocky asked.

"OH dear," said Mr Hawkins. "A silly rabbit ran out from the hedge, right in front of my van. I had to swerve to avoid hitting it and so I ended up in this hedge, and I can't get out. All the boys and girls will be waiting for me on a hot day like this. They will be wanting their ice cream, and I don't know what to do."

Rocky said, "I have an idea. You wait here and I'll be back soon." It didn't take Rocky long to run the mile back in to town. He saw Lassie and shouted to him "Gather up all the dogs in the town, and meet me here in five minutes."

"OK Rocky," barked Lassie. Lassie started to make a howling noise, holding his head up high while he did.

Soon all the dogs heard the howl and knew to come to where Lassie was. Rocky had run up to the house.

"Come on Betsy, Mr Hawkins needs our help."

"Oh not again!" said Betsy, but she got up immediately when Rocky said that someone needed help. They both ran down into the town to meet Lassie and the other dogs. By now there were about twenty dogs, all running down the road to help Mr Hawkins.

When they reached the van, Rocky barked. "Who brought the rope?"

"Nobody mentioned a rope," said Lassie, "So nobody brought one."

"Don't worry," said one of the dogs, "I know this place. There is a beach just over the other side of the road. We can collect some long pieces of seaweed from there, because it is very strong like rope." The dogs ran to the beach and lifted as many pieces of seaweed as they could. (The long pieces of strong seaweed are called Kelp.) Each one put a piece of Kelp around the van's front bumper, and started to pull. The dogs pulled for all they were worth. The van moved a little, then slide back again, even further than before.

"Oh no," said Rocky. "Try again. This time Mr Hawkins and I will go to the back of the van and push." He barked again, "One - Two - Three - pull with all your strength."

The van moved. "PULL, PULL, PULL," shouted Rocky. The van was almost out of the hedge. "Just one more PULL," Rocky barked again. With a bump the van came back onto the road.

"Thank-you all so much." said Mr Hawkins. "Jump on everyone, and we will go to Whitehead and deliver the ice cream to the boys and girls." When they saw the ice cream van coming along the road all the little boys and girls jumped up and down with glee. Mr Hawkins was so pleased with what the dogs had done for him that he gave each of them the biggest ice cream he had. Each one had a chocolate flake in it, and it was all for free! (Of course he used special dog chocolate.)

All the boys and girls also got the biggest ice cream possible, with real chocolate on it. Everybody had a great day. The children were happy, as the ice cream cooled them down. The dogs were happy because the children were happy. As for Rocky and Betsy, they both ran off with their ice cream to eat in the garden while lying in the sun.

"I am not doing anymore today," said Betsy, "I'm just going to soak up this lovely sunshine."

"Me too!" said Rocky as he licked at his ice cream.

The next few weeks were quite uneventful for Rocky and Betsy. Mostly they played in the sand or the forest, if they were in Castlerock or around the rocks if they were in Whitehead. One day Rocky had found a big fish called a ling hiding in one of the rock pools. He soon caught it in his mouth and was eating it for lunch when he heard someone call his name.

"Hi Rocky!" the voice said. "Remember me?" Rocky looked up. It was Richard and Jack. They had come back from London. Rocky assumed they were here on business.

"Well Rocky, how are you keeping?" asked Jack.

"Great!" Rocky barked, as he ran across the rocks to meet them.

"And how are you father?" The two dogs chatted for a while and then Rocky asked them why they were over here this time.

"You don't know?" asked Jack.

"No I don't. I thought maybe it was business."

"We have come for your Birthday. You will be twenty-one years old on Saturday."

(Rocky was just three years old in human years now - that equates to twenty-one years in a dog's life.)

"That's only three days away. Your mum and the girls wanted me to ask if you would come with us to London to stay for a while, and have your birthday with us. Of course Betsy could come too."

"I would love to!" said Rocky. "But what about Mal and Mue? They would miss us."

"Don't worry, Richard said, I have already spoken to them and they would love to come as well. So shall we all leave on Friday?"

"Yes! Yes!" Barked Rocky. "I have always wanted to see London."

Betsy was also very excited. "Is it a long way to London?" asked Betsy.

"About 1000 miles," said Jack.

"Do we have to walk or swim to get there?" asked Betsy, this time a little bit hesitant. She was not too

sure if she really wanted to go if she had to walk all the way.

"No. Don't be silly," said Jack. "We will be flying." Betsy looked very worried. She looked at Rocky and cried "But I can't fly! I will be left behind."

"Oh Betsy! Don't you worry your little head about that? I will take care of everything," Rocky reassured her.

Friday soon arrived and everyone had their cases packed and ready to go to the Airport. Mue was fussing around the house saying things like "Have you all got your tickets? And what about your warm clothes, if it gets cold?"

"Oh stop fussing, Mal told her, let's get going or we will miss the plane." Richard took them all to the airport in a taxi. Rocky and Jack both sat on the front seat looking out of the window, taking note of all the other dogs and cats as they passed by.

"I would love to chase that cat," said Rocky.

"Well don't you dare!" barked Jack. "I am getting far to old now to chase cats," thought Jack. Mal, Mue, and Betsy sat quietly in the back seat. Betsy still could not understand how she was going to fly

all the way to London.

"Wow," she thought, "One thousand miles. It must be almost at the end of the earth." They all arrived safely at the airport. Richard checked in the cases, and then they all went for some breakfast. It was still very early, only about ten o'clock. The plane was due to leave at eleven thirty. After breakfast they heard the announcement.

"All passengers for the London flight please go to gate number two." Soon they were boarding the plane. Betsy could not believe how big it was, and couldn't understand how it could fly when she couldn't.

"It can fly because it has wings, like a bird." Rocky told her.

Betsy turned to Richard. She asked "Does it fly all by itself?"

"No." said Richard "It has a pilot."

"Oh that's ok then" piped in Rocky, "I know Pilot. He is a friend of mine from Whitehead. His owner is Bob, a ship's Captain. I wonder if he is with him?" Rocky puzzled.

Just then the Pilot announced. "Please fasten your

seat belts. We are about to take flight." "OH!" Betsy said, "I am frightened." "Don't worry." said Rocky, Pilot is a very sensible dog. He never gets into any trouble."

The plane roared down the runway and thundered into the air. When it was above the clouds the noise was not so loud, and everybody settled back into their seats to enjoy the flight. Betsy asked for a cool drink, and the stewardess brought her a special glass with some ice in it. She was now enjoying the experience of looking down at the sea, and land many miles below her.

After an hour, the Pilot came on the loud speaker again. "Seat belts on please. We will be landing in London in approximately ten minutes." The plane landed, and they had all enjoyed the trip. Betsy loved it so much she wanted to fly back and forth all day.

They took another taxi to Richard's house, where they were all to stay. The taxi came into the road where Richard lived, and standing at the door to greet them was Rocky's mum, Bea. Rocky could also see his two sisters - Jas, and Bell. He ran to greet his mum and sisters. Everybody was asking questions all at once. Bea was so glad to see Rocky again. Rocky introduced Betsy to his mum and sisters. Richard introduced Bea and the girls to Mal and Mue.

"Well we have a big surprise for your birthday Rocky,"

"Oh what it is?" barked Rocky.

"We are going to see the Queen of England later today. She is coming from Balmoral in Scotland, to stay at her palace in London, and we will see her as she passes. We can also show you around London."

"Great!" said Rocky, I would love to see the Queen."

Betsy started dreaming, "Imagine seeing the Queen! I must get my hair combed, and put on a new bow at the front."

The Queen was due to pass by at or about three pm. Rocky and all the family were able to get to the front of the crowds, who had come to see her majesty. Some were waving flags, others were shouting, "God save our Queen." They saw the shiny black limousines coming down the road.

There were policemen everywhere. Some on huge

horses; others even carried guns -all to protect the Queen. Rocky got a great view as she passed. Betsy was up on Richard's shoulders, to see better, as she was quite small. Suddenly there was a great gust of strong wind. It blew the Queen's hat right off her head, and down the Mall. The policemen were running after it as fast as they could. Other people joined in the race to catch the Queen's beautiful green hat with pink flowers on it. Every time someone was just about to catch it, the wind blew it a bit further along the road. It was as if the wind was playing a game with them. Rocky thought, "Ok," that's enough," and started to chase the hat too.

Rocky was faster than any of the policemen or the other men at running. He was even faster than the wind! Rocky soon caught up with the hat, and grabbed it between his teeth. He held it gently, because he did not want to bite through the Queen's hat. "She might put me in the Tower of London for ever if I did that!" Rocky thought.

He ran passed all the people who were now trying to catch him, because he had the hat. Rocky ran right up to the black shiny car which was carrying the Queen. He took one huge leap, and landed on her knee. The car stopped with a jerk. The policemen and all the guards pointed their guns at Rocky.

"Don't shoot!" barked Rocky. "I am only giving the Queen back her hat." The Queen told all the guards to put away their guns. Then she said, "Well thank you very much. This is my best hat, and I would have been very sad to lose it. What is your name? You're a very brave dog to jump into my carriage like that."

"His name is Rocky," shouted a little boy from the crowd. "I know him from the pictures in the newspapers. He saved two boys lives, and he won the fastest, toughest, dog race in the whole world. We all love Rocky. He is the best dog alive."

"So you are the famous Rocky!" said the Queen."

"Yes I am your majesty."

"I have read all about you in the papers too. What are you doing here in London?"

"It's my birthday tomorrow," announced Rocky.

"Is it indeed," said the Queen. "Well you and all your family are invited to the palace tomorrow for a big celebration. We will have a super party for

your birthday."

The next day they all dressed up in their very best clothes. Betsy went to the dog hairdressers and was looking her very best. Rocky was just Rocky, and enjoyed meeting the Queen's two Corgis. (Although he thought they were a bit too snobby for him.) It was all over far too quickly, and everybody had to go home. The next few days Richard showed them all around London. Everywhere Rocky went people recognized him, and wanted his autograph. At the end of the week they all said their goodbyes. They were going home by ship this time. Richard took them to the port and waved as the ship pulled out to sea.

Rocky and Betsy were standing together on the deck as the ship passed by Whitehead. "Doesn't it look different from the sea?" said Betsy.

"It sure does," answered Rocky, And it won't be long until we are over there looking out to sea again".

ROCKY AND BETSY GO TO THE CIRCUS

About one hour after passing Whitehead the ship docked in Belfast. Mue and Mal were the first ones down the ramp, followed by Rocky and then Betsy. They were all chatting about what a great time they had in London. Mal called a taxi and asked the driver to take them all to Whitehead. On the way past Carrickfergus, Mue noticed a sign at the side of the road. It read; BIG CIRCUS COMING TO TOWN.

Mue asked "Who would like to go to the circus?"

The two dogs barked together "Yes, yes, please."

"I have never been to a circus" said Betsy.

"Well I did run pass one a long time ago," said Rocky. "There were all sorts of animals, large ones and small ones. There were also some very large cats. I would not like to chase one of those cats!" Betsy wondered what a big cat would look like.

"Right that's settled" said Mue. "I will get the tickets for next week."

Rocky and Betsy were very excited, and just could not wait. There was another three days to go until they were going. Each day they would play circus. Rocky would pretend to be a big horse or a lion. He would try and growl as fiercely as he could to sound just like a lion. Betsy pretended to be a monkey, and would roll over in the grass as if she were doing tricks.

Then the day came. Mue told Rocky and Betsy to be on their best behaviour or they would be brought straight home again.

As they came closer to the big tent they could hear the music. It was loud and cheerful. There were lots of stalls around the big tent. One was selling ice cream, another was selling candy floss, and many others had souvenirs of different kinds.

Rocky heard a man's voice over the loud speaker.

"Everyone with a ticket to see the greatest show on earth please line up here." Mue walked across to where the man stood. Rocky followed, and then Betsy.

"Please take your seats," announced the man.

Soon the tent was full of people ready to watch the

circus. The ring master came out. He had a big whip with him, and every now and again he would crack it in the air.

"Welcome everybody," he shouted. "We have a great show for you all tonight."

"I hope it's better than last night" shouted one little boy who was sitting in the front row with his dad. The little boy was called Jimmy. He had been to the circus the night before with his mum. Jimmy was cheeky and spoiled. He was rude to everyone, but his mum and dad would never scold him about it. The ring master glared at him, and thought to himself, "Not you again!"

First came the monkeys, Rocky and Betsy laughed and laughed at the tricks they could do. The little boy tried to throw things he found on the floor at the monkeys to put them off their tricks.

Rocky thought "I wish I was close to that boy. I would give him a nip in the backside every time he was bad." Next came the clowns. Then it was the turn of the elephants. They paraded around the ring, sometimes putting their two front feet on the back of the one in front. After the elephants the ring master announced that he wanted everybody to be very quiet. He went on to say, "We have some of the fiercest lions now coming into the ring. They can be very nervous, so please be very quiet."

The lights dimmed and only the centre of the ring could be seen. Rocky turned to Betsy and whispered, "These lions could eat you and me, and everybody else in the tent if they wanted to".

"Oh," said Betsy "I am so frightened."

"Don't worry I will hold onto you. I won't let the lions eat you all up for dinner." Rocky told her. Hoping that he didn't have to try stopping a lion from doing whatever it wanted to.

Just as the huge lions were entering the ring, the cheeky little boy in the front row pulled out a whistle from his pocket. He blew it as hard as he could to frighten the lions.

The first lion, which was the biggest of the lot, reared up onto its back legs and roared. It roared so loud that the whole tent shook. The lion then pulled its trainer across the floor and broke free. It ran straight to the boy, roaring all the time. The little boy just stood and cried. The huge lion jumped right over the top of him, then jumped over the next six seats, and ran out the door of the tent.

Everybody was scattering in all directions, trying to get away from the lion on the loose. The keeper had control of the other lions in the pack, and soon put them back into their cages. But the big one called Lawrence, had by now run away from the circus and into the nearby countryside.

"WOW," said Rocky "Did you see that lion go? I never thought anything so big could run so fast. It was a bit funny watching all the people dive for cover."

"Well he is a fierce lion, that's what the ring master told us," said Betsy.

"Yes, he certainly looks fierce," Rocky replied. "I would not like to meet him in the fields after dark, or even in the daytime," thought Rocky.

The police and the army were now arriving at the circus tent. They all had guns with them. Rocky heard one man, who seemed to be in charge telling the others "Shoot it on sight, as this lion is very dangerous. It could devour a man in five minutes."

Another said, "You're right. It's a real killer. No mercy from anyone for that lion." Some days passed and Rocky and Betsy could hear the helicopters still flying overhead looking for the lion. "It's probably well away from here now," said Rocky.

"Yes" Betsy agreed "If I were him I would be heading for the mountains and hiding up there."

"Well come on then," said Rocky "Let's go and play in the mountains. Let's pretend I am the big lion and you are looking for me." Rocky ran into the fields and up into the mountains. He hid in a hole in the ground. Betsy was looking everywhere for him, when suddenly something made her turn around.

There was the big lion staring straight at her. Betsy just froze. She just could not move or make a sound. She was paralyzed with fear. Rocky was directly above her on a ledge. He could see Betsy, but not the lion.

"Come on Betsy", Rocky barked. "Why are you just standing there?"

The big lion then spoke to Betsy. "Is he your friend little dog?"

Betsy could just about nod her head. She was so frightened she was almost sick. The big lion looked at her shaking, "Don't be frightened" he said in a very low voice, "I will not do you, or your friend any harm."

"You mean you won't eat us?"

"No. I won't eat you or your friend, but I am hungry."

"I am a very friendly lion" he went on to say, "Everyone thinks I am vicious, because I happen to be big and look fierce." By this time Rocky had come down from the ledge. Betsy introduced Rocky to the lion and told him, "He is really a very friendly lion, who has been misunderstood."

"My name is Lawrence," said the lion. "I can be very nervous, and when that cheeky little boy blew his whistle it frightened me. In the circus they always switch out the lights when we come on. That's to frighten the people, but I am afraid of the dark, and when I heard that noise I just had to get outside into the light."

"Well, you are in trouble now Lawrence," said Rocky. "The police and the army are going to shoot you on sight, because they say you are a fierce lion and would kill and eat a man in five minutes".

"I have never killed anything in my life," protested

Lawrence.

"I have always been with the circus, since I was a cub, and my owners have always fed me. I would not know how to kill anything. Now this means I can't return, because if the police or army see me they will shoot me."

"That's right," said Rocky. "You certainly do have a problem."

Just then Betsy turned to Rocky and said, "Shush! Do you hear that noise?" They all stopped talking and listened. "There it is again, like a moaning sound," whispered Betsy.

"Yes I heard it too," said Rocky. "You hide in that cave Lawrence; we will see what is making the noise. It seems to be coming from over there."

Rocky and Betsy crept steadily across the rocks until they came to a small opening. They looked down and saw a man in a policeman's uniform lying on the ground. Beside him was his gun. Rocky told Betsy, "Wait here, I will climb down and see what is wrong with him."

Rocky came up beside the policeman. He licked his face and the policeman looked up, grabbing his gun.

"Don't shoot," shouted Rocky. "I am a dog."

"I thought you might have been that lion which escaped from the circus. It's a man eater you know."

"Oh is it?" said Rocky. "Anyway, what's happened to you?"

"Can't you see I have broken my leg? I fell from that ridge. Can you help me?"

"Well I could not carry you, because you are too heavy for me. It's also getting dark, and by the time I could run back into town it would be very dark, and I would not be able to find you again."

"I will die if I have to lie here all night," moaned the policeman. "Can you do anything to help me please?"

"Well," said Rocky "I do have a good strong friend, who, if you asked him nicely, might carry you back to town."

"Please go and get him," shouted the policeman.

"What's his name anyway?"

"It's Lawrence," said Rocky.

"Now where have I heard that name before? I just can't remember," wondered the policeman. Rocky told Lawrence what he had to do.

"Are you off your head? Are you mad Rocky?" said Lawrence. "Carry a policeman into town? He will shoot me on sight."

"Oh no he won't," said Rocky, "because I hid his gun when he was not looking. Now listen to me. You carry him into town and everyone will know you are not a fierce lion, that you are a friendly lion, who just got a bit frightened by the whistle. You will be able to go back to the circus, and everyone will love you. It's the best chance you have Lawrence."

"You're right Rocky let's do that." The policeman nearly fainted when he saw Rocky, Betsy and the lion coming down the path towards him. He went to grab his gun but couldn't find it.

"Oh dear, are you all going to eat me?" he whimpered.

"No," said Rocky. "This is my friend Lawrence. He is a gentle lion, and he is going to carry you back

into town on his back."

"Me on his back? I thought I would be in his stomach by now." The policeman climbed onto the lion's back. They soon came to the town. All the people just stood and stared when they saw the lion carry the policeman to the hospital. The policeman told everyone about how good and gentle Lawrence really was. Lawrence went back to the circus, and after that he was allowed to give all the little boys and girls a ride on his back.

However there was one he would never allow on. Can you guess who that was? Yes, you are right, it was Jimmy the cheeky little boy who caused all the trouble.

THE MAGIC FOREST

Rocky was playing on the beach at Castlerock by himself. Betsy had stayed in bed, as she was not feeling too well. He was chasing the seagulls as usual, when he noticed a funny little green piece of cloth floating on the sea. Of course Rocky went to investigate. He had to swim out a little bit to catch it. He grabbed it in his teeth and brought it back to shore. It was a small scarf - maybe for a dog or someone very tiny. Rocky started to play with it, pulling it along the beach, until he heard someone shouting,

"Hey you! What DO you think you are doing with my scarf?" Rocky looked all around, he could not see anyone.

"Who are you?" the voice asked.

"I am Rocky."

"Well answer me Rocky. Why are you pulling my scarf up and down the beach? Do you know it took me three years to knit that scarf, and it is my very best one?" The voice sounded very cross now.

"I just found it in the sea," said Rocky. "I am very sorry. I did not know anybody owned it."

"Of course somebody owns it. And look at me when I speak to you!" said the voice.

"I would, but I can't see you anywhere."

"I am down here between your paws." Rocky looked down, and there was a tiny man all dressed in green.

"Wow," barked Rocky. "You're a funny little man, and why are you all dressed in green?"

"I do not think I am funny at all. I am a very serious person. I dress in green because I live in the magic forest. Seeing as I am dressed in green I can hide in the grass when humans come along and they can't see me. They think that if they catch me, I will grant them any of their favourite three wishes, just so that they will let me go free. How stupid these humans are. First of all they don't believe I exist, and then they think that if I do exist, I will grant them anything they want. Well, are you going to give me back my scarf or not?"

"Oh yes of course," said Rocky.

"What is your name? And tell me please where this

magic forest is that you live in?"

"My name is Norman. I am a Gnome. In fact I am King of the Gnomes this year." Norman put his scarf back on again, now that it had dried in the warm sun.

He went on to point out - "The magic forest is right over there. You should know it well Rocky. I have seen you there, with your master many times, walking in the forest. You have run right past me often. You see, that's why I wear green."

"I have never seen any magic in the forest," said Rocky.

"That's because you don't know where to look, and you don't know what you are looking for."

"Will you show me?" asked Rocky.

"I will, because you did rescue my scarf, but I am not getting into this three wishes thing. It tires me carrying out all this magic in one day."

"You really are magic then?" asked Rocky.

"No I am not magic, but I can do magic," answered Norman.

"Wow!" said Rocky aloud. "I would love to be able

to do some magic". "Well, come with me and I will show you the magic forest. You can meet some of my friends. It just so happens that we are all having a party tonight in the forest. It's my birthday. I am just two hundred and thirty today."

"What did you say?" asked Rocky in disbelief.

"Oh yes, we Gnomes can live over a thousand years, so I am really still quite young. What age are you Rocky?"

"I am three now, and I had my birthday with the Queen of England."

"Yea, Yea," said Norman, "And I had the Pope at my birthday last year." Rocky could sense that Norman didn't believe him, so he just let the subject drop.

Soon the two were in the forest. "Yes I do come here all the time," said Rocky, "but I don't see anything different."

"You will if you can be quiet for a few minutes," replied Norman. Rocky did as he was told and kept very still. Suddenly he heard a voice. It was a very creaky old voice, like the branches of a tree in the wind rubbing together.

"Where have you been Norman?" the voice asked. Norman turned to the tree beside him and said, "I was on the beach looking for my scarf. It had blown off in the wind. This young dog, called Rocky, very kindly retrieved it for me from the sea."

Rocky looked startled, "A talking tree?" he said. "Yes," said the tree "We all talk to each other, just like the grass and the flowers do. Why do you find that so strange? You dogs talk to each other, and so do humans."

"But you have no mouth," said Rocky. "Look a bit closer and open your eyes and ears in the forest, and you will see we have all the same things as you do. We just can't run the way you can. But you can't grow as tall as us, or see all over the forest like we can," said the tree. "And another thing Rocky. Please be careful where you do your pee in future, last time you did it all over my boots; sorry I meant my roots."

"OH, I am so sorry," said Rocky, wondering where he should pee in the future. Seeing as everything was alive around here, he was sure to offend someone.

At that moment Rocky saw coming up the path, an array of coloured lanterns. Carrying them were about a hundred Gnomes, all in different coloured dress. Some were in green, like Norman. Others were in brown - they were from the heather clan. Another group followed wearing white, and they were from the daisy clan. The yellow ones were from the dandelion family. Rocky was amazed at how many there were.

"We are here for the party," they said to Norman. Soon they all had barbeques going, and the smell of burgers and sausages was drifting through the forest. Even some of the ducks and the birds joined in, although it was well past their bedtime. Rocky was having the time of his life.

"I wish Betsy was here to enjoy this with me," he thought. Rocky was eating a packet of meaty crisps, when a gust of wind blew them from his hand and into a tree. He had been really enjoying those crisps, and there could have been about half a packet left. He tried to scramble up the tree, but it was too high and too dark to climb now. Then someone said, "It's going to be morning soon. We had better get back to our homes before the humans start walking in the forest." Rocky agreed

that it was time for him to get back to his house too. He did not realize how late it was.

The next morning Rocky awoke about eleven o'clock.

"Well sleepyhead," said Betsy. "You slept well last night. In fact you kept me awake most of the time with your snoring."

"I did not," protested Rocky "I was out at a party all night in the magic forest, with a gnome called Norman who is over two hundred years old." Bea started to laugh.

"You silly dog, you have been dreaming." Rocky told his story to Mal and Mue who both assured him that it was only a dream.

"There are no such things as Gnomes, or talking trees!" Rocky then decided that indeed it must have been a dream after all. But later that day when they all took a walk into the forest, Rocky looked all around, and to his astonishment he saw a half packet of meaty crisps high up in the branches of a tree. The tree gave a shake, and down fell the crisps right at Rocky's feet. He rubbed his eyes and looked again. This time he thought he saw the tree wink an eye at him.

"OH," said Rocky, to himself, "It is all true. I had better not say anything to anyone, because they will not believe me. But I know what I saw."

So always remember - Be very quiet while you are in the forest, and listen to the trees rubbing their branches together. If you keep your eyes wide open you might ...you just might ...see their faces in the bark.

ROCKY AND THE AVALANCHE

They spent the rest of the week at Castlerock. On Sunday they started to head back to Whitehead again. Rocky and Betsy loved both places. There was so much to do and so many different places to play in each town. The beach and the forest in Castlerock, and the rocks at Whitehead. They both loved to watch the trains at Castlerock, and at Whitehead.

Rocky would sometimes chase the trains, along the path beside the track. He would run as fast as he could, but was never able to keep up with them. All the drivers knew Rocky, and he knew all the drivers. There was driver Sam, who lived not far away from Rocky in Whitehead. Then there was his brother John, and their father Tom, also train drivers.

Rocky always wanted to drive a train, but he knew it would never happen. As they approached Whitehead they saw lots of flags on the lamp posts, near the promenade.

"What are all the flags out for?" Rocky asked.

"I don't know," answered Betsy. They were all lovely colours. Some were red, others white, and some others were blue. They stopped and asked a person standing by the road side about the flags.

"Didn't you know the Queen of England is due to pass by soon, in the royal yacht Britannica, on her way to visit the lord mayor of Belfast."

"Ah, I see now," said Mue. "We were away for a while and missed the news." They drove the car on down the road until they came to the shore. The Queen's magnificent yacht was just sailing by, and everyone was cheering. Once it had passed Mue said "Right you two, it's time for supper and off to bed. You have both had a long day."

Mue was right. Rocky and Betsy were almost asleep. They took their supper, a drink of water and some special dog biscuits they both liked. "I am going to play trains in the morning," Rocky announced, just before he fell fast asleep.

After their usual sausage breakfast, Rocky and Betsy went down to play on the grass beside the railway track. They were very careful not to go onto the track, as they both knew that this would be very dangerous indeed. Rocky ran up and down the path, pretending to stop at different stations, while Betsy pretended to be one of the passengers. She would ask Rocky what way the train was going, and at how many stations it would stop. They were having great fun, when suddenly there was a tremendous noise behind them. It seemed to go on and on like thunder, only a lot louder. Rocky covered his ears because of the noise. He also had to shield his eyes from all the dust. Betsy was very frightened.

"Oh Rocky," she shouted "What was that?"

"I don't know," said Rocky. "We will have to wait until the dust clears to see what has happened. The noise had now stopped and all was quiet again. The dust cleared slowly in the gentle wind. Rocky could see a little now, and he was horrified by what had happened.

"Look Betsy. Look over there. All the rocks have fallen down and blocked the railway tunnel. The driver will never know to stop on time and his train will crash right into them. The accident will kill everyone on the train."

"Oh dear Rocky. What can we do?"

"I don't know what we can do. But I am certain

that the express train, which will be travelling at full speed, will be here in less than fifteen minutes."

"Oh Rocky! We must think! Think! Think!"

Rocky put his head between his paws. (He did this sometimes when trying to do some fast and serious thinking.)

"I have an idea, and I just hope it works, if we still have time. Follow me Betsy. Run as fast as you can." Rocky and Betsy ran onto the promenade, where they had seen all the flags the day before. Sure enough, some were still there, lying on the footpath, and scattered around the roadway.

"I have seen the train guards do this sometimes. They wave red flags to let the drivers know something is wrong. If we gather all the red flags we can and put them further back along the track. The driver should see them and slow down." The two dogs quickly gathered six red flags each, and started to run towards the track again.

"We have only five minutes left. Hurry Betsy! Hurry! You start here with your flags. I will run a bit further down the path." Rocky dropped one flag, and then ran on a little further, where he dropped another. He continued to do this until he

had only two flags left in his mouth. Then he saw the express coming along the track.

"OH! NO!" Rocky barked. "I hope we are not too late." The express was hurtling along at a hundred miles per hour. It was the fastest train in Ireland and it was full of passengers, all coming home after a hard day's work.

Little did they know that the line was blocked just ahead, and that a very big crash was about to happen if they kept on going.

Rocky could just see the driver. It was Sam, and John was there with him. The express always had two drivers - the same way as an airplane has a co-pilot, in case something happened to either one of them.

Rocky held the red flags in his mouth, and stood on his back legs, waving his head from side to side.

"What on earth is that, waving a red flag?" said John. "It's Rocky." shouted Sam, who was at the controls at the time. "Look more red flags on the track further down! I think Rocky is trying to warn us of some danger ahead. Right, no more time to waste. Put all brakes on full NOW!" The huge train began to shudder. The wheels locked

and skidded along the track, sparks flew from the hundred massive wheels. Rocky thought it was like a fireworks display. The noise was terrible. The train skidded on and on along the track.

"It's too late," shouted Betsy. "The train is going far too fast to be able to stop on time." Now Sam and John could see the avalanche ahead of them. Huge rocks filled the tunnel and lay all over the tracks.

"We will be killed!" said John.

"I don't think this train can stop on time."

"It will have to. IT must!" shouted Sam, as he pulled even harder on the brake lever. The train was slowing down now, and when it was just about the length of a baby's foot from the rocks - it finally stopped. The passengers were all jumping out of the carriages. They were all terrified. Sam and John came down from the train and looked at the rocks scattered all over the railway line.

"Well Rocky, and Betsy. If it were not for you two, everybody would have been killed here today. What can I do to thank you both?"

Rocky announced, "I know what I would like."

"What's that then?" asked Sam.

"I would like to drive the train someday."

"ME TOO!" barked Betsy.

"Right, you both deserve a reward. I will talk to the train controller, and explain to him that you pair are being allowed to drive the train to Belfast and back."

"Hurray!" barked Rocky and Betsy. Sam and John honoured their promise of letting Rocky and Betsy drive the train.

First was Rocky who sat up proudly in the cab, and drove the train all the way to Belfast. Betsy was a little more nervous. She sat on Sam's knee at the wheel, on the way back. But Sam did most of the driving.

THE FAMILY GO TO FRANCE

When they arrived back home they told Mal and Mue all about it. "You two have had some great adventures together" said Mue.

"Between here and in Castlerock. I remember the time you won the greatest race, and you Betsy won the best looking dog competition."

"Yes," said Rocky, "It was all good fun, but most of all I liked the magic forest."

"Oh please Rocky," said Betsy "That was only a dream."

"Well maybe to you, but it was real to me."

"Come on now, you two, no arguing," Mue interrupted, "Everybody can believe what they want to, as long as they do not force others to believe it also."

"Yes that's right." said Rocky. "Remember the time when old Jake and Jacob locked me in the shed? Everybody believed I was the one stealing all those sausages."

"Well I didn't," barked Betsy, "I knew you would not do such a thing."

"And neither did Mal or I" said Mue.

"Anyway, after all this excitement we have had lately I think it would be good if we all went on a holiday. Maybe to another country for a change. We could go to Spain or maybe to France. Would you two like that?, I know that Mal would" said Mue.

"Would we be going in a big airplane again?" asked the two dogs.

"We would," answered Mue.

"We would love to go," they both barked together.

"Then that's it settled. Pack your cases and let's go." They decided to go to France, as that is where Mue was born. She promised to show them all around Paris, and the surrounding countryside. Rocky and Betsy were sitting at the window seat as the plane took off.

"Bye Bye Ireland for a while" said Rocky, "We won't stay away for too long - I hope."

The plane touched down in Paris airport about

two hours later. Everyone enjoyed the flight, saying how good the pilot was, and how beautiful all views were from the sky. Mal and Mue collected the bags, then headed for the underground train, which would take them all into Paris.

Rocky and Betsy had never been on a train that went under the ground before, and both thought that this might be very exciting. However, to their dismay they found it really boring. There was nothing to see from the windows, except when they saw half lit rocks with wires dangling from the sides as the train rushed passed.

Soon the train came into the daylight again. "We are here" announced Mue. "This is where I was born." Rocky and Betsy were looking out at all the different buildings. In the far distance they could see the Eiffel tower. It stood above everything. Rocky thought that it nearly reached the clouds.

Everyone was getting off the train, so the family joined the queue to show their tickets at the exit. Rocky heard a dog barking in the distance. "What a funny bark," he thought. Then he heard the people talking to each other. "What a funny way to speak. I can't understand a word they are saying."

"These are French people with French dogs," explained Mue. "They do not speak the same language as we do in Ireland."

"Oh I see," said Rocky, wondering why everyone could not speak the same language. It would make things a lot easier for all the people in the world. Soon they arrived at their hotel called The Grand. And grand it was too. Mal and Mue went upstairs to their room, while Rocky and Betsy were shown to their kennels outside in a large garden. There were about ten other dogs staying at the hotel. Each one had a little stretch of grass and a kennel of their own. The kennel had a very comfortable blanket and a little heater.

"This is real luxury," barked Betsy, "And did you see the dog swimming pool? It looks wonderful!"

"I did, so maybe we will go for a swim before dinner. H'mmmm talking about dinner," said Rocky, "I wonder what's on the menu?"

"Probably frog's legs or smelly snails," said Betsy.

"From what I have heard about French people they eat all sorts of weird things."

"Well I don't care. As long as there is plenty of it

and it tastes good." Rocky tried to talk to the other dogs, but only one spoke English. He was a long dog called a Dachshund. Rocky thought he looked like a very long sausage.

"Yes I know what you're thinking Rocky. I don't like being this shape either. Some people call me a sausage dog."

"Well" said Rocky laughing, "Seeing as it's a very hot day, I will call you a hotdog,"

"Oh very funny" said Danny (that was the dog's name.) Danny the Dachshund.

"Where are you from?" asked Betsy. Although Danny could speak English, he did have a funny accent.

"I am from Germany" he announced proudly, and over there is my towel - on the best seat by the pool. I got up early this morning to make sure I got that one!"

"Ok," said Rocky, "We won't touch your towel or your seat, but we are going swimming now. Would you care to come with us?"

Betsy was first into the water. She barked, "Come on you two, the water is lovely and warm." Danny was next. Rocky decided he would show off a little, and went to the highest diving board at the side of the pool. At the bottom was a sign, it was written in French DANGER! PLONGEOIR TRES HAUT, (which means DANGER! VERY HIGH DIVING BOARD) but he went up anyway. He climbed and climbed until he was at the top. Rocky looked down, "Gosh it is a long way down," he thought. "I can't dive from here."

He saw everybody looking up at him shouting "Come on. Jump Rocky, Jump!" Betsy was frightened and had her paws over her eyes. She could not bear to look. She was shouting "Don't jump Rocky. It's too high!" Rocky was a bit frightened. He did not know what to do. He was really scared to take the plunge, but if he walked back down now he thought everybody would laugh at him.

"Oh why do I have to be a show off?" he said to himself. Suddenly a big black cat appeared at the side of the pool. It looked up at Rocky and started to grin. The big cat turned around and waved its tail at Rocky, as much as to say "You can't catch me. I dare you to try."

Rocky knew he should not chase cats after what

had happened before. But he just could not resist this one. "That French cat is asking for trouble," he thought. Rocky dived into the water. All the people roared and clapped. "What a brave dog!" they shouted. But Rocky did not wait to hear them. He jumped straight out of the pool in seconds. The cat looked startled for a moment.

"How did he get here so quickly?" she wondered, as she sped off as fast as she could. Rocky was right on her heels. At one time Rocky caught the cat by the tail with his teeth, but had to let go again. The big cat could run fast, but hadn't reckoned on how fast Rocky could also sprint. It ran to the right and then left. It turned into alleyways. It jumped over boxes and bins.

The big cat was beginning to wish she had never started to mock Rocky. She was getting tired and Rocky was catching up on her.

"I will have to do something, or that dog will catch me." thought the cat. With one last bound of energy the big cat leapt onto a bin, and from there onto a high wall. The next move was to climb up a drain pipe and then onto the roof of a house. She lay there exhausted. Rocky wasn't able to climb the drainpipe. He sat on the ground, barking in

frustration. The big cat looked over the edge, and said, "Don't worry Rocky. You gave me the best chase I have ever had. It was great fun. But my dinner is now ready and I have to go."

Rocky watched as the cat jumped from roof to roof on its way home. "OH No" Rocky said. "I have done it again I'm lost, and this time in strange city, I can't even ask the other dogs for directions. I am silly! I said I would never chase cats again. They always get me into trouble." It was getting dark and Rocky wandered about the streets. He tried to speak to other dogs, but they just laughed at him, because they could not understand what he was barking about. He found a bit of chicken somebody had thrown into an entry because it was quite a bit past it's sell by date.

Rocky was very hungry now, and was glad to eat anything. He thought of the lovely hotel he was staying at, with the warm kennels. Now it was getting very cold as night fell. "I wonder what was for dinner?" he thought. "Maybe duck or roast pork? Oh," said Rocky, "I really hate cats!"

Rocky woke the next morning, and climbed out of the old sack he had found in the entry. He had not gone too far before he heard a voice shouting behind him. Rocky could not understand what the man was saying. The man suddenly threw a net over him, and trailed him into a van with strange writing on the side. Rocky was trying to protest, and tell the man who he was, but without success. He was taken to the French dog pound in Paris. Here he was put in with many other dogs, who thought Rocky was very stupid as he could not speak their language. Rocky did find out that one of the dogs spoke a little English and so he and Rocky became firm friends. The little dog was a poodle, called Trouble.

"That's a odd name," said Rocky. "It is what my owner said about me.

"Just Trouble," so he left me in here. Weeks passed. The people were good to the dogs. They kept them warm and well fed, until someone would come along and take them home- just like at Benvarden. Trouble would teach Rocky some French.

He said "You will need to know the language if you have to stay here in France."

Mue, Mal, and Betsy, were all very sad. They could not find Rocky, but had to go home, as their holiday time in France was finished.

Two more months passed by, and one day a fine gentleman came into the dog's home. "I'll have that Jackabee" he said. "He looks like a grand dog. What is his name?"

"He is called Rocky," said the attendant. The man was English. "I think I have met this dog before somewhere. Yes, now I do remember. He was at a party with the Queen. I was there too, as a guard when I worked for her Majesty. What is he doing in here?"

The attendant told the gentleman all about Rocky, and how he had now learned to bark in French.

"Yes indeed. A very smart dog," said the man. "I will take him back to his rightful owners." The guard took Rocky to the airport and paid for his ticket. He then phoned Mue and Mal to let them know Rocky was safe, and on the plane home.

Everybody was at the airport to meet him when his plane landed. They all shouted and cheered and had a banner which said -

WE LOVE YOU ROCKY - GREAT TO HAVE YOU HOME AGAIN!

Written on it.

"It's great to be home again," barked Rocky. Then he said "Je me demande combien d'autres aventures Betsy et moi vont avoir." (This means in English - "I wonder what more adventures Betsy and I will have in the future.")

THE END. (FOR NOW)

Written by. MJT ABBOTT.

THE TALKING TREES

IN THE MAGIC FOREST

ROCKY HAVING FUN

PLAYING WITH TIM

PLAYING WITH A BALL

PLAYING IN THE SNOW

PLAYING IN THE SURF

PLAYING WITH OLLY

ROCKY CATCHES A FISH